Blade of Prophecy

Wind of Destiny, Volume Nine

AJ Cooper

SANCTON
THE BLESSED ISLES
Eloesus
RIVER SULIS
PALLISTRIX
ISTEROS
ARCTOS
100 mi.
200 mi.
300 mi.
400 mi.
500 mi.
AGATHÉ
TIGRIS
IOGHEIRA
STRAITEIRA
THÉNAI
THENOA
KERSEPOLI
KERSICA
KORTHOS
KORTHICA
ORACLEA
TEN CITIES
THARTA
THARTICA
ARKADIOS
THEMURIA

THE RECKONING

Elena Kaiaphon stood stiff as her guests approached.

She was in the threshold of Kronos' temple, before the great marble stair.

Her underlings had told her of a vast army arriving in Thénai's harbor, promising service in the Old Gods' name.

One by one, dark shapes emerged from the winter fog, some dressed in hoods, others with their heads bare, but all in black.

At their fore was a giant of a man, and as his face took shape through the vapor, Elena Kaiaphon had to suppress a scream.

This was the man who called himself Pereon, the leader of all these tens of thousands of Old Believers. He was not at all what Elena Kaiaphon expected. He was a monster.

Parts of his face had receded, leaving bare his gums and his yellow teeth. There were lesions on his arms and on his legs.

Elena had witnessed such deformities before, when flesh flies were left unchecked. She had fled the city when the southrons attacked, but now she remembered, she remembered it all. This Pereon had led the invasion of Thénai; at that time, he had pledged allegiance to the Kersican League. He had been the city's enemy.

Elena remained a patriot, but she did not care about Pereon's past. He would serve her… he would be a tool in her hands, for the Thenoan League, for Kronos… but above all, for herself.

"Welcome," Elena Kaiaphon said. "You have come, bearing swords, for the day of battle. It is here the fate of the world is decided… who shall rule? The Old Gods or the new?"

Pereon knelt before her, and the hundreds behind him followed.

A horn pierced the silence of the morning. Every day, every hour, more Old Believers arrived. The New Gods did not stand a chance.

PHILLIPIDĒS AND THE FIELDS OF PARADISE

A FABLE

When Phillipidēs was in the prime of his life, returning a victor from the Megarine War, a beggar declared as he walked by, "Surely you shall enter the Fields of Paradise!"

At that moment the underworld opened its jaws and swallowed the beggar whole, leaving a great rift in the ground.

Phillipidēs looked into the great gap and wept. None could enter the Fields of Paradise but heroes, and who was a hero only the gods could determine.

—Amalchio

COUNCIL ROOM, INNER FORTRESS, CHOROS, THENOAN INLET

Khloë and Phalco had taken refuge in Choros. They had set up headquarters within the depths of its highest, innermost fortress, expecting to remain alone, but each day, more government officials from Thénai filtered in.

It was late one morning, just as the winter storms had begun to rage, when a figure darkened the doorway.

He wore a chiton as white as snow, and over it a blue sash. A sword was buckled to his side.

Khloë knew him by his shape, by his gait; though he was a silhouette, she knew instantly this was Teucer, Speaker of the Assembly, the highest ranking member of the government after Dioscouro's expulsion.

At the sight of Teucer, memories returned to her, memories of those panicked hours as she fled the city.

The Assembly of the People had voted to expel the city's leader, Dioscouro; and in an instant, a great riot had erupted, plunging the city into chaos. The Old Believers had taken advantage and seized control.

"Teucer," Khloë said. "It is good to see you."

Teucer stepped into the light. He was smiling. "Khloë. You are safe."

"Safe," Khloë said, "but worried."

"As are we all," Teucer said.

~

That night, they set out candles in the Council Room, on

tables and on sconces. Outside, the wind wailed like a ghost, and the sound of the pelting rain echoed through the Inner Fortress. They gathered blankets for the demiarchs and politarchs who had survived the city's hour of peril; in total, they numbered twelve, including Khloë and Teucer. It was a pitiful showing, but the holy gods—in their wisdom—had apparently graced a few with life. Khloë and Phalco's boldness had served them well, but as for the others, hundreds had fallen to the sword. They had been butchered like cows, by the Old Believers, by the irate people of Thénai, and otherwise. Here they were: Thénai's provisional government, twelve in number, cast aside on an island.

"Dioscouro is dead." Teucer had wrapped a blanket around himself, but he was seated at the head of the Council Table. "I witnessed it for myself."

"Dead?" Khloë cried. "Dead?"

Although she had grown to despise Thénai's former leader, although she now believed him to be a coward, a cretin and an opportunist, the news did not bring her any joy. One time, long ago, she had held deep respect for him. One time, long ago, she had considered him a friend.

"The crowd trampled over him," Teucer said. "Strange, isn't it… the mob wanted him as archon, and yet it was they who ensured he never would be."

After the House of Assembly voted to strip an archon of his power, it was customary to send him naked, in only his underclothes, into the city streets. Perhaps the crowd did not recognize him in such a state. Or perhaps, in the fury of the moment, they had not paid attention.

Either way, it was an ignominious and perilous end for a man with such a long and fruitful career, who had ascended to the heights, to the city's most coveted position. It was exactly the end that he deserved.

"We must leave soon," Khloë said. "The seas will grow unnavigable."

"And where shall we go?" Teucer said.

There was no safe place for them in Eloesus.

The Old Believers were in control. Their reach now extended into the entire nation.

~

In the morning, Khloë was awoken to a frantic knocking on her door.

She opened it quickly.

"My lady, my lady," the servant girl said. "Come with me."

She dressed quickly and followed the servant out of the Inner Fortress, down many sets of stairs, through many gates, to the least fortified part of Choros: the harbor.

A boat idled there, tied to the docks. Khloë had never seen a boat of its kind before. Its prow was carved in the shape of a dragon, and its sails were brilliant yellow and red.

Standing there, next to it, was a woman in a crimson hood. "My lady Khloë," she said in an accent Khloë didn't recognize. "A message for you."

"From whom?" Khloë said.

"Theron," the woman answered.

THE WESTERN HILLS, ISTEROI KINGDOM

The storms had ceased, and for the first time in a long time, the sun was shining, and the sky was a clear blue.

Geon, fearing attacks from the Isteroi king, had drawn Herodota out here.

In this woman, forty years old, the hope of Eloesus would rest.

He looked upon her in the sunlight. The many months of sorrow had worn her down, and Geon could sense it within her. There were wrinkles in her face, and worry marks on her forehead. Even now, she lacked spirit; she lacked belief. She had a faith, once, but it would be difficult, if not impossible, to restore.

In the days after Thénai fell to the southron hordes, her fellow priestesses had been put to the sword. The monstrous leader of the southrons, whom Herodota had called "Pereon," had sent her away alive as a witness, to tell others in surrounding cities and towns what would happen if they crossed him.

"Herodota," he said. "We must act quickly. If you are to restore the priesthood…"

Herodota, even now, was weary. "What are you, Geon? You never told me."

Geon extended his wings. He wished he knew. He wished he understood what had gotten into him. He wished he knew why he had completely changed. In a way, he did know what happened. He had ventured to the Stygian lake; he had drunk the Stygian water. A star had fallen into the waters long before, imbuing it with its power, and Geon had drunk deeply of it.

But *what* was Geon? That was a question even he did not know. He just knew that he had begun to transform, that his power was growing every day, until he was bursting with it. What was he? He did not know… and perhaps he never would.

"Do not worry about me," Geon said. "You have a task ahead of you, Herodota… a serious task. Eloesus' fate is up to you."

Herodota said nothing for a while. Eventually she turned, walking away from Geon, up and down the hills.

~

The hills were bright green after the recent rain, and though the air was cold, signs of spring were everywhere. In the smattering of trees dotting the hills, birds had begun to nest. Soon, the flowers would bloom, and the travails of winter would be forgotten.

"Herodota! Herodota!" Geon called after her.

Eventually, she stopped her walking. She turned to face him. "I must go back, Geon. This is a fool's task. It always has been.

"I must go back to Arctos. I am a refugee and nothing more."

She removed her black wig, the ceremonial attire of Amara's priestesses, and set it on the moist grass. Her bald head was bare for everyone to see.

"I am sorry," Amara said. "Why should I serve a goddess like Amara? If she is powerful, she allowed my friends to be slaughtered like lambs. If she is powerless, she is not worth serving."

Even seeing Geon's radiance and splendor, she resisted. He had drawn her out of her dwelling place in the city of Arctos; he had convinced her once. Now he had to ensure she remained in his care.

She had stopped her walking; a seed of faith remained inside her. Geon needed only to water it. Then, the priesthood would have its restoration. Then, the temple would have its sanctification… and the abominable thing that now lay within the sanctuary would be expunged from memory.

Much had to happen. There were many things to be done, and very little time.

~

That night, they fashioned a fire out of logs and twigs. Geon set it alight.

Leaving was a necessity; Herodota had eaten just about all of Geon's waybread.

Though Geon, amid his transformation, no longer needed nourishment, there was a limit to what he had brought along. Eventually, they would need to find human habitation and purchase food. The scorn of the people was a danger Geon had to face.

Herodota had donned her wig once more. Her wavering continued, and for now the priesthood won out. Her azure gown, the ceremonial garb of the priestesses, was now stained with mud, and frayed along the edges. Yet some of the light had returned to her eyes; some of her sorrow, Geon sensed, had begun to wane.

"If I were to restore the priesthood," Herodota began, "I would need junior priestesses.

"And the monster… the monster who slew me… he may yet be alive. He may yet hunt me down. You know why he set me free, don't you?"

Herodota had told this story many times before. Try as she might, she couldn't shake the fear she had of the southron military commander she called Pereon. At night, when she slept, Geon noted frequent nightmares. Was it him she was dreaming of?

"I will protect you," Geon said. "I've been sent for this task. I will guard you, Herodota, for as long as I live… for as long as I am here with you.

"If you are to reform the priesthood, we must act quickly. We must find initiates. Where shall we go?"

"I... I think," Herodota started. "I know a woman. Unmarried, as far as I know. She left for a mountain village. She had tired of Thénai. She was my parishioner... one of my wards.

"Each Third Night, she brought a ewe lamb to sacrifice on the altar. She was pious. She was devout. She truly believed."

Herodota looked away.

"Geon... I don't think..."

She was still hesitating. "Where is this mountain village?" Geon said. "We must leave at once."

"Brindos is its name," Herodota said. "It is south and east of here... but I do not know the way."

"To Brindos we go," Geon said. "We leave tomorrow morning."

THE GOLDEN ROAD, OUTSIDE PHALKIS, KERSICA

Taicho had been in Axander's company for many weeks, but this was his first glimpse of Kersica.

Phalkis lay many miles outside the capital, but it was built with defense in mind, with great golden walls studded with towers. The gate was broad and reinforced with steel, but what lay outside of Phalkis drew Taicho's attention most of all.

This was the first sight of Elehoi Taicho had witnessed.

Elehoi, the Kersicans called their slaves. Once they had been free men, living as citizens of Eloesus and enjoying all the rights they were afforded. But some point, far back in their family line, they had fallen victim to the Kersicans' conquests.

When the citizens of Phalkis resisted their captors, they were sold into bondage, into a reduced state, with no rights to speak of or no hope.

Several hundred of them were outside Phalkis digging a trench.

They were blond and brown-haired, dark and light of skin, with shovels. All were emaciated and appeared underfed. Beside them, a dozen or so Kersican hoplites watched. Their red capes identified them as free Kersican men, all of whom were trained for war.

Taicho had learned all of this back home, all the way across the sea, in the city of Lornadion. As a member of the Thenoan League, the citizens of Lornadion had been taught all about the rough edges of their enemies. He wondered if there were rough edges to Thénai, but he'd never heard of any. Thenoans had banned slavery altogether, and they would never sell an Eloesian into bondage, not even a Kersican. Taicho spat toward the city as they passed by.

He walked alongside Pythio, a true prince, the son of a king. Pythio was the only reason he was alive; their captor, Axander, intended to exact a ransom from Pythio's father. They were only days away from the sea-port, where the letter of extortion had been sent.

Phalkis eventually disappeared behind them, and the sounds of shovels and the shouts of slave drivers faded away into nothing.

Taicho had grown weary over these weeks of marching, but he had gained endurance; and he had gained determination. He had sworn to himself that, if he ever escaped, he would fight his way back into the Thenoan League, and he would either help conquer the Kersicans or perish in the attempt.

~

That night, the air cooled, and a gentle wind was blowing.

Axander, standing tall in his headband, watched as his soldiers fashioned a fire from twigs, branches and leaves. Over the weeks, he had grown gruffer, ruder, with something of a cruel streak.

It was no wonder; Taicho had witnessed the cause of this change firsthand. Selling Pythio was not his first task; no, he had failed at the first one. His attempt to slay the "monstrous" creature Geon had come to a ruinous and embarrassing end.

"You! Taicho!" Axander snapped. "Make yourself useful!"

"I'll gather logs," Taicho grumbled. It was as good an excuse as any to leave camp.

The gentle wind helped wash away some of Taicho's

stresses. Even in winter, the heat had only barely relented in Kersica. There had been no rain for many days.

In the light of the moon, he made out a small patch of forest a short distance away. As he walked, he began to think, to wonder, how he could possibly escape. If Pythio was ransomed, they'd be taken back to his father's kingdom. And from there, how could he ever return to Thénai? From there, how could he ever rejoin the League he had sworn allegiance to? From there, how could he take the fight to the Kersican armies? How could he bring sweet vengeance to the Elehoi of Phalkis?

The moon was shining, a waning crescent, a brilliant white against the stars. The forest had a wintry silence; the crickets did not chirp, nor the cicadas. Amid the pines and cypresses, Taicho was the only thing stirring.

He began to search for broken branches and started bundling up twigs and whatever would set alight.

The trees surrounded a stagnant brown pool, whose surface was caked, in parts, with dark scum. A stag was lapping up the water not far away; it turned its black eyes to Taicho, locking gaze with him.

Then suddenly, it bolted away; and footsteps echoed, the sound of breaking twigs and pine needles.

Taicho dropped the logs and kindling and drew his dagger. "Show yourself!" he cried. Would he become an Elehoi?

The long shadows, cast by the forest, made each sway a tree-branch seem like a person, or a demon of hell.

But eventually it was someone of Taicho's size that showed his face.

It was Pythio. "Sorry," he said.

"Have you come to help me?" Taicho said. He stooped down to grab the dropped logs, twigs and kindling.

Pythio had never shown such warmth before.

"I thought we could talk here… where no one could hear us," Pythio said.

It was a risky proposition, even alone. Axander's henchmen would never ease up watching their captives; each movement of theirs would be watched and carefully examined.

"I have a confession, Taicho," Pythio said.

Taicho's stomach dropped. "What is it?"

"I am not a prince," Pythio said.

"But… but…" Taicho stammered. He did not want to believe it. How could they possibly escape if he had lied? "Your necklace…"

He had a necklace with a gold chain—a pendant of an egret, with diamonds for its eyes. He had tattoos written in Khazidean pictograms.

"The necklace, I stole," Pythio said. There were tears in his eyes. He had never shown any emotion before. "I am a thief. A liar. Nothing more than that. We'll be executed if we do not escape! We must run, now!"

"We can't outrun them," Taicho growled.

"One thing I said was true," Pythio said. "I am from Khazidea. From Sarkopoli. But I was forced into the Thenoan army like you…"

Taicho had never felt so betrayed. He had been lied to… given false hope. He would never look at Pythio the same again. His opinion was lower of Pythio than before his string of falsehoods began. He was not a prince but a thief, but worse than a thief, he was a liar, a deceiver.

"How could you…" Taicho murmured. In a moment, all his hope had vanished.

"We must run!" Pythio no longer sounded his confident self. "We must run, now!"

"We can't outrun them!" Taicho cried again. "They'll kill

us. Is that what you would have happen? You fool! You cretin!"

But his lies had saved them; his lies had prevented their execution. Axander had been ready to kill them both, but Pythio's silver tongue had convinced him. He was a prince, Axander thought. And Pythio had proven it... a necklace of gold no commoner could afford, and tattoos that appeared royal in character.

In the end, Taicho should have thanked Pythio; but he wouldn't. He wouldn't. Not now. Not while rage still burned inside him. His hope was gone. He would never escape Axander alive.

"Grab some wood," Taicho said. "Or else, we'll look suspicious."

~

That night, the fire blazed, a raging and towering inferno, and smoke wafted high up into the air.

"Well, Pythio," Axander said, the flames gleaming in his eyes, "you are a gift from god. I have informed the Kings of Kersepoli about you. They know all about it. The leaders of the Kersican League!" He was smiling brightly. "A ransom will not be enough. We will put the Prince of Khazidea to good use... your father will be hearing from us soon."

HARBOR, CHOROS, THENOAN INLET

Khloë had welcomed the emissary into the heart of the fortress.

In the evening, they set out a table—she, Teucer, and all the demiarchs who remained—and prepared a feast.

On the porch outside the Inner Fortress, the sea was visible, and the evening sun cast all in red and gold.

She was dressed in crimson, and had tied her hair in braids. She was pallid and was no doubt foreign. Her accent was thick and difficult to discern.

They still had not opened the letter, which she claimed was from Theron. She insisted they not open it until she departed. The letter, bound up in a wax seal with the letter "Th" imprinted upon it, was addressed to Khloë and no one else. Perhaps, in the end, he truly did care for her.

Servants brought out a platter of roast lamb and set it upon the table. Another came bearing bottles of wine, another crystal cups, another sweetcakes, another oil, another salt and various seasonings.

"You are so generous," the woman said, who called herself Strychë. "I shall bring back news of your hospitality to my homeland."

"And where, may I ask, is your homeland?" Teucer, Speaker of the Assembly, asked.

"Sail for weeks, to the west, and you may find it," Strychë said, "if the storms do not take you, and the tritons do not strike."

"Dys?" Teucer said.

The peninsula on the western terminus of the Middle Sea was the furthest place in Eloesian knowledge. Not even the geographer Laocon had gone further.

"Beyond Dys," Strychë said. "In the ocean. If you follow the patterns of birds, you may find Telantë. Those who find it call it the Isle of Serpents, but it is so much more.

"Theron found us. He earned the favor of our king. He is beloved of our people. And I departed with him. I was his comforter."

A spark of jealousy formed in Khloë. "What do you mean, comforter?" she snapped without thinking.

Strychë only smiled in return. "I have come bearing the letter," she said, "but I am headed home. Telantë is my next stop. But I have done this one last task for Theron.

"I believe, in my heart, that he is a hero… that he is favored of the holy gods."

Strychë spoke the truth, but Khloë did not need her to know. She could hardly wait to open the letter. But Teucer was insistent on treating Strychë royally. No expense was spared in the hopes of gaining a foreign ally.

~

Dusk faded to night, and the moon, a waning crescent, glistened over the whitecaps. A great wind was stirring up the sea, but torches were burning, and the feast showed no sign of waning.

Strychë, they soon learned, was the daughter of a prince, a woman who had followed the hero Theron out of love, against the wishes of her father. She had dwelled with him for years, and it was Theron who had sent her away, back to her family.

"But before you return," he said, "go to the city of Thénai, and bring this letter to the amazon Khloë."

"I learned the true government was at Choros," Strychë said. "I thank the holy gods that you are alive, Khloë. Else, my task would have been fruitless."

Khloë smiled. Over these hours, she had grown to like this Strychë, so regal, so courteous and refined, but not arrogant. She treated everyone with respect. She treated everyone kindly.

Remains of food lay untouched on platters.

Strychë stood up. "Thank you for your hospitality," Strychë said. "I have grown to appreciate you all… and now I must go. The stars will guide me home."

Teucer stood up. "Farewell, Strychë."

He had not gained an ally in the war, but he had gained a friend. They all had.

She left the letter, sealed in wax, on the table.

Once she had gone, Khloë broke the wax seal and allowed the letter to unravel.

The ink was black, and the letters were perfectly formed. Theron evidently had a scribe in his mountain redoubt:

DEAREST KHLOË:

I THOUGHT ABOUT YOUR JOURNEY TO FIND ME, AND YOUR WORDS WHEN YOU ARRIVED.

I KNOW THÉNAI IS IN TROUBLE. I TOLD YOU I DO NOT BELONG. AND I DO NOT.
BUT I AGREE TO MEET YOU.

AT COUNCIL OVERLOOK, ON THE FIRST DAY OF SPRING, I WILL BE THERE. I PRAY YOU WILL BE AS WELL.

—THERON

Khloë could hardly contain her joy. She was beaming when

she turned to face Teucer and the other members of the government.

"Ah," she said. "My friend… my friend… I will see him soon."

CITY GATE, KERSEPOLI

Taicho held his breath as he passed through the gate, and crossed the threshold into the city he dreaded. He was fully aware of the danger he was in.

Pythio's lies had brought them here. Pythio's lies would get them both killed, unless Taicho could find a way to escape.

~

Kersepoli was not at all what Taicho expected.

The streets were paved white and immaculately clean. The buildings were pristine, with plaster walls and bright red roofs. There was no garbage discarded, no remains of chamber pots.

But it was empty.

The only people he saw passing by the way were women with very small children, toddlers who could scarcely walk. Young girls were there as well, and young women, but he did not see a single man.

Taicho suspected he knew why.

In Kersepoli, all citizens, all free men, were warriors, taken from their mothers as soon as they could talk. In camps, they were trained as nothing more than killing machines, to be heedless of the elements, to build up endurance, to care for nothing and think of nothing but war.

That was what the teachers in Lornadion claimed. Back home, Taicho had not believed them; but now he did.

There were no men in the main thoroughfare in Kersepoli, only women and children.

"Axander!" a woman cried. "Hail Axander!"

The hero of Kersepoli had not quite been given a hero's welcome, but the people of Kersepoli recognized him instantly.

Eventually the thoroughfare, perfectly straight, paved in white stones, opened up into a vast city square.

It was similar to Thénai's in shape, but it was plain, the same color as the road, and only a handful of merchant stalls were set up. In one corner, a fishmonger was selling the freshly caught fish of the day. In another, a clothier was selling gowns and dresses. One, in the center, had trinkets and toys on display, but there was vast space between them. Commerce was not a Kersepolan specialty; slavery and robbery was. They trafficked in violence, not in goods and wares.

The Royal Palace faced Kersepoli's city square. The vast monument was crafted from sandstone, and colored red.

At either side of the door, hoplites were posted, with red horsehair crests on their helmets and swords and shields in their hands.

Unlike the citizens of Kersepoli, they did not break rank to greet Axander, or shout his name. They only inclined their heads and kept silent as he walked by.

But they did let him by, into the most exclusive of places, where only the most valuable of people could enter unmolested: the home and office of the two most powerful men in the world, the Kings of Kersepoli.

~

For the most powerful men in the world, their thrones were bare, completely without ostentation. They looked more like chairs than thrones, built of wood, without ornament, and set up on a raised stone dais. These did not look like the seats of powerful kings.

It was King Phaedrion who greeted them; King Leonaras was far afield, fighting the Thenoan League somewhere, seeking to take advantage.

He was not dressed for war; his chiton was plain, dyed a deep scarlet. Around his head he wore a diadem of purple cloth, wrapped around and tied in the back. He was somber as he entered, and did not smile or greet Axander.

Seated upon his throne, King Phaedrion examined Axander first, then Taicho, and last Pythio.

"This is the princeling you spoke of," King Phaedrion said. "He is a Khazidean if I've ever seen one."

Slender and swarthy, with a hint of copper to his skin, Pythio was clearly a foreigner, but foreigners were common in Eloesus, represented in the highest echelons of city governments. He did not belong to the Eloesian nation, but many foreigners had become citizens… many foreigners, even back home in Lornadion, had come to its temple asking absolution, bringing offerings to the civic gods, and were registered in its book.

"I will send a message to King Anakh and King Astarthe," Phaedrion said. "Surely, you miss your father. Don't you, Anakh?"

Taicho could hear Pythio gulp.

"Anakh?" Axander said. "His name is Pythio."

"I thought all kings of Khazidea had the name 'Anakh,'" Phaedrion said.

"They do," Pythio said, "when they are enthroned. But at birth they have another name."

Pythio was the best liar Taicho had ever heard; the lies came pouring off his silver tongue, and he always spoke with confidence. He was nothing if not convincing.

King Phaedrion looked at Pythio questioningly.

Axander proffered Pythio's broken necklace. "Here is the proof his father needs."

King Phaedrion balked. "If King Anakh needs proof from a King of Kersepoli, he is a greater fool than anyone could think," he said. "My seal will be enough evidence for anyone.

"Pythio… you are my ward. But who… who is this? This fellow Eloesian?" He gestured to Taicho.

"He is my father's cupbearer," Pythio lied for Taicho, who could never be so convincing. "He has served my father since birth. His name is Taicho."

King Phaedrion was gazing at Pythio, examiningly, probingly. Perhaps, he was not nearly as naive as Axander. After all, he was well educated, experienced in the world at large, and less susceptible to deception. No doubt he was wise and cunning; one had to be, to assume the kingship of Kersepoli and remain in that position for so long. Few kings lasted more than two years. At least, that was what had been taught by Thenoan teachers in the market square of Lornadion.

"You are a captive," King Phaedrion said. "And you are a captive of the Kersican state. Yet you are a royal, and you will receive the treatment of a Kersican royal. Your prison will be the best we offer."

~

In the "royal" chamber King Phaedrion had chosen, the walls were bare and unfurnished. There were no curtains in the windows, and the sun was glaring. The bed was a cot on the marble floor, with not so much as a pillow. In one corner was a wooden table, with two stools.

Taicho wondered if the king's chamber was no better.

In the corner opposite the table was an iron pot. No lavatories were afforded to guests, even those who received the "royal treatment."

"Axander," Taicho said. "There is only one cot." He had just noticed.

Behind him, a guard's voice echoed: "Royals receive the royal treatment. Not so 'cupbearers.'" He was on the verge of laughter; perhaps, to him, it was amusing.

~

The guard led Taicho down a set of narrow hallways. The sconces on the wall illuminated bare stone walls and plain marble floors, without decoration. Eventually, an arched doorway led them down a staircase, below ground.

The guard nudged Taicho along, and Taicho reluctantly followed.

Below, in this subterranean area, the floors were not of carved marble but instead of rough flagstone with uneven footing. Twice Taicho tripped, and twice the guard, who was bearing a torch, refused to help him.

Along the coarse, rocky walls, chains with collars were tied. In one dark corner, Taicho spotted an old man with a beard who was restrained in this very fashion; he was emaciated, with his ribs showing, and was singing under his breath.

That would be Taicho's fate, unless he found a way to escape. For now, he had to obey orders, and hope and pray that Pythio's silver tongue would lead them both out of imprisonment.

The guard, smiling, motioned to one of the unused chains.

Taicho heaved a sigh, muttered curses under his breath, and walked over. An unsettled feeling had come over him. The worm of worry was twisting in his gut. He had heard great tales of the Kersican's cruelty in the market square of Lornadion, and he had seen nothing to discount them.

The collar was fastened to Taicho's neck, and without the illumination of the guard's torch, he was left in total darkness.

~

The sound of the old man's singing rose above the silence. Taicho stopped his weeping, a moment, to listen.

"Ió Amara in her heavenly home,
Ió her servants in the clouds,
Ió her servants, swords glist'ning, shields shining
Ió Amara come to earth,
Ió Amara come here,
Ió descend, descend Amara, descend!"

Taicho knew the motherland well enough to know which cities which served which gods. Kersepoli, appropriately, revered Tyros lord of war. Korthos revered Nix, goddess of secrets, more than the others. It was Thénai who revered Amara, queen of battle, above any else in the pantheon.

Could this old man, weary and hungry, be a fellow Thenoan?

Perhaps, Taicho was not a Thenoan in the truest sense of the word. But he had fought on Thénai's behalf. He had borne her sigil on his shield.

"Who are you?" Taicho's voice was faint; in his hunger and thirst, he had lost much of his strength. He did not know if it was day or night, whether the sun had already set or risen once more. Here, it was always night, always completely black.

The man's voice, when he answered, was weak and wheezing. On his first attempt, he fell into a coughing spell.

Eventually, he managed to speak. "My good man… who are you? You sound young."

"I am Taicho," he answered. "And who are you?"

He could not see a mote of anything, only hear the sound of the old man's breathing, and of rats skittering across the floor.

"You are too young for this fate!" the old man said.

His accent was not Thenoan, but from elsewhere, perhaps the colonies.

"I curse the day I was born, Taicho!" the old man continued. "And what a strange name you have…"

"I am from Lornadion," Taicho said. He had grown weak from hunger, and the mere act of talking sapped most of his strength.

"I am from Dys," he continued, "from Dys, far across the sea… I never intended to fight for the motherland, but I was forced into it."

"Pity, pity, Taicho of Dys," the old man said. "Do you want me to tell you a secret? I know one."

"What is your secret?" Taicho answered.

"I am not a prisoner. I am not a prisoner at all."

SIARIS, THE NORTHERN SHORE, OUTSIDE THENOA

Khloë disembarked from her ship in the driving rain. The wind was blowing and the air was bracing in its coldness. Winter, in all its somber glory, had arrived.

She turned to bid farewell to the sailors, who had agreed to ferry her away from Choros despite the danger of the seas.

Draped in a winter cloak, and clutching Theron's letter in her hand, she watched as the ship was pushed away from its dock and set free into the open waters. She waved, but the sailor did not answer; they were too concerned with their safety, too concerned with the danger of the waves and the ocean currents.

Khloë had a long journey ahead of her, one which would be full of danger. Traveling in winter, amid the muddy roads, would be a difficult proposition, and especially on the path she'd be taking, up into the mountains.

Council Overlook, where Theron promised to meet her, lay impossibly far away, in the Oracle's territory. Overlooking the valley of Arkadion, it was etched into the side of the Mount of Prophecy. There, the four cities of Thénai met in ancient days, back when the nation was unified. The nation had not been unified in hundreds of years. Once, Korthos, Thénai and Kersepoli acknowledged the sovereignty of the King of Tharta; but where was Tharta now? Neutral in all affairs, she had receded as a great player in the world. Her conduct in the Southron War had not been forgotten. Thénai and the Kersican League now vied for the position that Tharta once held by rights.

Khloë walked off the dock, into the makeshift village that served as a port. On the doors of the inn and the houses, wreaths were hung, and throughout the streets trees glimmered with candles. She had almost forgotten it was Yule, the celebration of "light overcoming darkness," whatever that meant. No doubt, in Thénai, commerce had ceased in recognition of the holiday, but here was Khloë, alone in her work. She had to get to Council Overlook before the turning of the season. She did not want to keep Theron waiting. She could not, and she would not.

~

On the dark Yule night, Khloë—using her collective savings—purchased a mare from the local hostler, an exorbitant sum of seventy-five *doukon*, paid in silver and gold.

The painted horse had bells on her ankles, and the name of Cadelita in honor of the horse goddess. She ate a small meal in the inn, a dinner of roast lamb and baked bread, and a small cup of spiced wine. She left when it was still dark.

~

When she crossed into the border of Thenoa the next day, she wondered and she worried what had befallen the capital. When she left, the Old Believers had stormed the High City, the House of the Archon was burning, and riots had consumed the streets. She wondered if the Old Believers had seized control. With ships ceasing their activity for the winter, little information had reached Choros. Teucer, the highest ranking member of the rightful government, was at a loss. Would the Strategoi of the Free and Democratic armies heed the word of a woman like Elena Kaiaphon? Khloë hoped not, but it was not out of the realm of possibility. She was of old blood, a fixture in the city scene, a woman of great prominence and known throughout the soldiers' ranks as a patriot and devoted Thenoan. They did not know she was an Old Believer, and they did not know the dark deeds the Old Believers committed. They had attempted to sacrifice the most precious human life of all, a young child. Had the word spread? Khloë hoped so, but she did not know.

The winding roads eventually led her, days later, onto a thoroughfare of white pavestones. This was the main artery of the Thenoan League, the pulsing heart of its commerce: the Golden Road.

Khloë was surprised at its business. Rattling down the road were dozens of carts, pulled by oxen, carrying heavy cargoes to the capital. Hundreds and hundreds of travelers packed each inch of the thoroughfare, some leaving but most headed west, toward the city proper.

The League had almost completely returned to normal.

She thought, with a note of dourness, that the riots had ceased, that Elena, queen of the Old Believers, had assumed full control. Somehow, the people of the Thenoan League did not mind.

When Khloë joined the Golden Road, headed east toward the mountains, she began to wonder and to worry. If Elena had taken the reigns of the League, would it continue to function the same way it had? Would she rule well? Would wealth return, all while the Old God sat in Amara's temple? Would the pantheon be forgotten, and mankind return to an age of ignorance? If the old belief remained, Amazonia would not escape its shadow. Perhaps, it would spread, to Tigris and Kolkis, to the capital cities and great towns, even Bythia, the small village Khloë had once called home.

As evening fell over the Golden Road and the surrounding

hills, Khloë found the first inn that would welcome her. Cadelita's bells jingled as she trotted toward the inn's yard.

A stable boy came out to greet her. "My lady amazon! Welcome to *The Northward Star*!"

The room was dingy, and in the darkness, soldiers — off duty — were chatting amongst themselves and rolling dice. In another corner, merchants dressed in purple were sipping wine and nibbling at their bread.

Inns were the mark of the lower classes; a rich man, a member of the elite, was expected to find lodging with one of his friends, or bring his own sumptuous tents and attendants. Khloë was reminded of this when she noted the clientele.

A woman garbed in a tunic was chatting with the innkeeper, no doubt a prostitute who worked for *The Northward Star*, an added benefit for guests. Khloë recoiled at the sight.

A servant came running up to Khloë. "My lady," he said. He removed the winter cloak from her shoulders. "I shall have this washed and dried by tomorrow morn. Shall I draw a bath for you?"

"No, no," Khloë said. "No bath is necessary."

"Do you have need of anything else, my lady?" he said.

"Food and drink," Khloë said, "and also… if I may ask… knowledge. Knowledge of the wider world, if you have any on offer."

~

For dinner, the inn served bread and roast lentils, the fare you would expect at a roadside establishment. With her food came a small pewter cup of wine, a weak red, clearly watered down. The inn had cost her six *thalon* and she had received a six *thalon* stay. The floor had a distinct slant to it, and parts of the wood had begun to rot away.

Her request for "knowledge" had apparently been ignored; knowledge was probably in short supply amid these ignorant folk.

Khloë watched as one of the off-duty soldiers went upstairs with the prostitute. The merchants, by now, had become raging drunk, and spoke and laughed boisterously together. The serving boy could not refill their glasses fast enough.

It was only then, amid the cacophony and the noise, that she noted a table, tucked away in a dark corner, and a man sitting in it.

He was dark of hair, with a beard in the manner of the southrons. He was staring at her.

Khloë looked away, startled. *Perhaps,* she thought, *I should go to bed.* She was not yet tired, but if she propped something against her chamber door, perhaps she'd keep safe.

She was getting ready to leave when the man in the dark corner stood up and began to walk over to her.

The light of the candles illumined a face that she recognized.

She gasped when she saw him, Hektor, the man she had met half a world away.

It was he who had led her through fen and field to Bastos.

Somehow, for some reason, he had followed her here.

When she had tried to find Theron the first time, she had needed a guide. This Hektor had been exiled from his city for reasons Khloë did not fully understand. This Hektor had been a priest once, then an Old Believer.

"Hektor!" she breathed. "Hektor! Hektor! What are you doing here?"

"Khloë. It is so good to see you," Hektor said in his colonial accent. "Although, I must admit, I have been following you for a while."

Goose-prickles formed on Khloë's flesh. "Following me?" Khloë said. "Why? Why?"

"Theron said you would be traveling on the Golden Road," Hektor said. "The roads are more dangerous than you know, my Khloë. Theron wanted to give you extra protection. And here I am."

Khloë noted, for the first time, a sword dangling from a sheath.

"You have made dreadful enemies, Khloë," Hektor said. "Ruthless ones." His voice had lowered to a whisper. "The road is not safe."

"You know Theron…" Khloë breathed.

"I always knew Theron," Hektor said. "He is the King of the Mountains. An avowed enemy of Old Believers. So am I."

The fear had vanished in an instant, dissipating like smoke. She felt much safer than before, much more at ease.

And he was right. Khloë had aroused the ire of Elena Kaiaphon, and her servants were no doubt everywhere, her eyes and ears, hiding behind every corner.

"So you were not who I thought you were," Khloë said. "You were an ally all along."

She had hired him as a guide; she had tried to pay him in gold and silver. She had thought he was an exile, a hermit and nothing more.

~

As the hour grew late, and the darkness deepened, the candles began to snuff out, one by one.

The drunken merchants had demanded more wine, but the innkeeper stridently refused and they ended up—unwillingly—

staggering to bed. The off-duty soldiers retired to their rooms. Soon, the only candle that had not blown out was Khloë and Hektor's. They remained awake and talking in hushed tones at the table, long after all the servants at the *Northward Star* were asleep in their quarters. Only the innkeeper kept awake with a watchful eye, making certain Khloë and Hektor behaved themselves.

Over these dark hours, she learned that Hektor had been in Theron's service for more than a year when Khloë arrived, that he had had no idea of her intentions, that he had had no idea she was Theron's friend. When she had sought to go to Bastos, the place where Theron had been last seen, he guessed she was merely another Old Believer who would fall to Theron's club.

"Over the years," Hektor said, "that had become his prime goal, his motivating force… old belief, on the rise all over the world, was what grieved him most. Old belief had resurged after a long dormancy."

Khloë had never known Theron to be a pious man. He had spoken little, if at all, about the gods in their heavenly home. If he had spoken of them at all, he had been dismissive, like the philosophers were. Yet no doubt many years away from Eloesus, many years away from his home, had taken their toll on him. Perhaps, he had changed. Or perhaps, he saw the Old Believers as a threat to the world's stability, a threat to princes and kingdoms, a threat to the fabric of society. And they were a threat, beyond the abstractions of the gods and religion. Look at what they had wrought in Thénai and the wider nation. Look at what they had done.

By now, they had eaten every crumb of bread and licked clean every bit of roast lentil from their bowls. They had drunk two cups, each, of the watery wine. It was time to depart for bed, and time, tomorrow, to depart for Council Overlook.

"We have a long journey ahead of us," Khloë said. "It will

be difficult. The Golden Road is long."

"We are not taking the Golden Road," Hektor said. "Even staying in this inn is more risky than I'd like. We cannot risk being seen. The enemies you've made, Khloë, are not only dangerous, they are more powerful and more widespread than you can imagine.

"We venture off-road, tomorrow, into the hills. It will be many weeks until we reach Council Overlook. Until then, Khloë, I will be your guide."

GREAT ARCTOS ROAD, BORDER OF THENOA AND THE ISTEROI KINGDOM

The mountains were behind them, the snowy peaks that were the source of the River Ister and the home of the High Grotto, but Geon—with Herodota at his side—knew greater things were ahead.

The town of Brindos lay in the Sky Mountains according to Herodota. In comparison, the Sky Mountains pierced the clouds, and Brindos—near the summit—was on the roof of the world.

Night had fallen, but Geon—a living candle—illumined the darkness, and Herodota had agreed to venture on. The night took away some of the danger of the road, and in the emptiness, Geon could pass through without molestation. The terror and hatred of the mortal world could not stop him when the roads were empty, when the night was silent and the darkness was complete.

Herodota ventured on because she had no choice and no place to go. He sensed her despair, her shattered faith as he walked. He knew she was full of doubt, without hope in the world, with only a spark of belief remaining. At times her old zeal resurfaced, but now she was walking without her wig; she had not shaved her head in days, and the hair had just begun to grow back.

She had become convinced Amara was powerless, that either she was distant and remote from the mortal realm or that the philosophers were right, that she was an idea and nothing more, a carving of stone, an image in marble. As Herodota's hope waned, so too had her zeal.

"My lord," Herodota said. She refused to stop calling him that. "I am getting tired."

Geon ceased his walking a moment and turned to face her.

They had arisen at dawn.

As Geon's transformation continued, sleep had become an annoyance, a bother and nothing more. He no longer needed it. He had not truly fallen asleep in more than a month, and now, more often than not, he merely waited through the night, hoping and praying that the sun would emerge and Herodota would awake. He had to remind himself of the weakness and powerlessness of humans, how they needed food and drink, how they needed rest, how their emotions got the best of them, cycling through hope and despair, sadness and joy.

"Shall we prepare for bed?" Geon said.

The road was completely empty. Far away, there was a campfire and tents pitched around it, but here, in this secluded patch, the darkness was complete save for Geon. As they drew nearer to the heartland, going off-road might be their only hope. But for now, the Great Arctos Road would have to do.

"Bed? No," Herodota said. "I must tell you, Geon… last night, I had a horrible dream."

She had not spoken a word in all this day of journeying. She had kept it close to her heart.

~

They went off-road, and as Geon wandered through a patch of trees, seeking kindling for a fire, Herodota began to tell him of what she had seen.

"I dreamed," she said, "of a king sitting enthroned. He was sitting amid the pillars of Amara's temple. They had stripped the sanctuary bare.

"The king wore a lion's skin on his head. He had returned from a far country.

"Then, as I focused on him, as I gazed upon him, I noted

he was dead."

The hero of the Southron War, Theron, was known to wear a lion's skin on his head. Geon, in his former life, had never seen him face-to-face, but he had heard much about him. People said he had slain a lion of supernatural strength which had crept up from the underworld, and scalped it with his knife. Geon had always assumed there was a more natural explanation for the mane's strange color, but he had kept quiet.

"You've been away a long time," Geon said. "It is only natural that you would dream of your old haunts. The temple. The sanctuary. And Theron, the hero of the Southron War…"

"That's the thing," Herodota said. "That's what disturbed me most. I knew Theron from long ago. It was not Theron wearing the lion's skin. Someone else was wearing it, and he was sitting enthroned in Thénai."

DUNGEON, ROYAL PALACE, KERSEPOLI

Days bled into nights, and the darkness of the dungeon was complete. At some point, the old man who had been singing had ceased talking altogether, and Taicho couldn't even hear the sound of his breathing. Perhaps, he was dead, or perhaps, when Taicho had fallen asleep, he had been taken. Either way, Taicho had become completely alone, chained to the wall, by himself in all his struggles and challenges. Pythio, the supposed royal scion, had a bed and chamber pot, but the thing Taicho desired most, the thing he wanted above all, was the blessed light of the sun. At night, he was overcome with nightmares, of fire and smoke and shadowy figures laughing in the flame. At day—or was it night—he strained to breathe and struggled in his soiled clothing.

"Taicho!" He recognized the voice of the guard instantly. "Sit up. Your rations…"

Within moments, a hunk of dry, moldy bread was shoved in front of his face, and Taicho, starving, ate it with relish. Next, a bowl of cold water was pressed to his lips, and he drank it all up recklessly.

"Thank you," he muttered under his breath. "Send Pythio my regards."

The guard laughed coldly. Once Taicho had slurped down every last bit of the cold water, he departed, disappearing into the darkness.

"Happy Yule!" he said.

Had so much time passed? To Taicho, it seemed impossible. He had been in and out of sleep, in and out of cold and darkness, and the days and nights blended together, becoming one. In his rusty chains, he had wasted away and grown weak. He could feel his ribs when he touched his chest. He would die here, if he did not find a way to escape.

He had wondered if there was some hidden weakness in the chain, or if somehow he could file it away. He had tried countless times to break free, but had had no luck.

"My lord!" Taicho cried.

The guard had stopped his walking. "Tell Pythio… tell Pythio… I am here. His father's cupbearer! I am here… his friend is almost dead."

The guard laughed in response, and his footsteps faded to nothing.

~

Taicho did not know if he had fallen asleep, whether he was dreaming or waking, when the noise of footsteps and chatter overwhelmed him. He only knew that he was suddenly wide awake, and a number of guards had surrounded him in the darkness. One was fiddling with his keys.

"What is the meaning of this?" Taicho cried. "What are you doing?"

There were loud curses, but eventually Taicho's collar clicked loudly, and fell free from his neck.

A guard gruffly grabbed his arm and jerked him to his feet.

They half led, half dragged him, out of the dungeon, refusing to tell him why he had been set free.

King Phaedrion was seated on his plain throne. Pythio stood before him, his hands cinched tight with rope. Axander was nowhere to be seen.

"Pythio, son of Gordios. Taicho, son of Philmedeos." At

Phaedrion's words, Taicho's heart exploded in his chest. He had been found out, somehow, some way.

"My father is Anakh, King of Khazidea," Pythio insisted.

"Lie again," King Phaedrion said, "and I shall cut your tongue from your mouth."

Pythio had begun to babble incoherently. "I'm sorry," he said at some point.

"Taicho," Phaedrion said, "you are no cupbearer, but the son of a fisherman. You are from the village of Lornadion in Dys."

"No, no," Taicho muttered. "It's not true. It's not true."

"Then why did you tell Gaion you were?"

Across a long span of time, he recalled, many days and nights ago—or was it months and years—the old man, singing the hymn of Thénai. Taicho had spoken rashly, telling him everything, of his origins. He had told him he was from Lornadion, that he was a Free and Democratic soldier.

He cursed Gaion, he cursed Pythio and all his lies, he cursed everything. He cursed the day he was born. He cursed the day Lornadion had announced its alliance with the Thenoan League. He cursed the motherland and all its problems, problems which had spilled the blood of innocents all around the world, problems which had drawn young men from colonies across the sea to perish in its wars. Why, he asked the holy gods in heaven. The holy gods were dead.

"Liars do not do well in Kersica," King Phaedrion said. "In Kersica, we do not suffer liars to live. Tonight, at sundown, you shall face your fate."

INTERSECTION OF THE GREAT ARCTOS ROAD AND THE HIGH ROAD

Crossroads were queer places.

From where Khloë stood, far from the inns and shops, she could see the humming of commerce.

She and Hektor were shrouded in the trees.

The ground had risen far from where they'd begun, and the air was crisp and cold.

Crossroads were said to be beloved by Nix, the goddess of secrets and mysteries. Crossroads were said to be her sacred space, where she worked her wonders. As Nix had one foot in the world of the living and one foot in the world of the dead, crossroads were part on one road and part on another. At crossroads, merchants going in vastly different directions converged, and towns popped up to serve their needs.

"Are you ready," Hektor whispered, "to go into the mountains?"

The wind was blowing, icy cold in character, and the recent rain had moistened the withered grass.

Khloë was not ready, nor would she be. Venturing into the mountains, in the dead of winter, was madness. But if she meant to meet Theron on the first day of spring, she would have to endure many hardships.

"I am ready," she lied, "as ready as I will ever be."

Darkness had fallen over the land. As Hektor prepared their camp, Khloë peered out into the lights of the town. She wasn't sure of its name, but she thought it was called Laoconia, after the explorer. On the doors of houses, Yule wreaths remained. The holiday was a month long affair, sometimes longer, and humans celebrated it with relish. Amazons also celebrated Yule, but only for one night, and with no such elaborate decorations. A few candles, lit in windows, and a few gifts, given to family and friends, were considered enough.

Hektor was building the tent, and clouds had rolled in to cover the moon, when a brilliant torch lit up the night far in the distance, bright white in color.

But it was not a torch.

Khloë gasped when she noticed it was a person, wreathed in brilliant light, with wings on his back and a blue circle of starlight around his head. Beside him was a woman, half-walking, half-staggering. She had a shaven head and a blue gown.

Who were these people, and what was that majestic creature?

All she knew, when she saw him, was that her heart was at peace, that the worries and cares of the journey seemed pointless in comparison to that splendor. Warmth and peace and love seemed to exude from his wings. And then he was gone.

OUTSIDE LAOCONIA, BORDER OF THENOA AND ORACLEA

Geon led Herodota around the town of Laoconia, trying his best to hide, though his light and glory lit up the night. He did not want to arouse the enmity and hatred of the Laoconians. He did not want to draw attention to himself.

Herodota, weak from exertion and from despair, would do well to sleep in the local inn, but Geon could not afford to let her out his sight. If he let her out of his sight, she could waver; she could abandon the priesthood and curse the goddess she thought had spurned her.

"Come with me," Geon whispered to her, as he began to circumvent the town.

The way to Brindos was ahead, on the High Road, off one of its many side paths.

But Herodota remained still, staring at the town of Laoconia. Tears glistened in her eyes. "Those wreaths… those candles… Yule. Yule. Oh, to be inside, near a fire. Oh, to give gifts… to receive them."

"You have a much greater gift to the world," Geon said. "A gift that will resonate through the centuries."

Clearly, the travails of the journey had begun to get on her. She did not smile, only wince and groan at the cold.

It was only a matter of days, and they'd arrive at Brindos. It was only a matter of days, and the priesthood could be restored. The work of the holy gods would not be without effort, but it would be worth it in the end… for the sake not of Eloesus, but for the sake of humanity, and the whole world.

CITY SQUARE, KERSEPOLI

The night was dark save the lights of torches, and the night was silent save the pounding of drums.

The executioner wore a mask with bulging eyes and a protruding tongue.

This was meant to be Nemesis, the judge and jury of the gods.

Axander stood to his left, King Phaedrion to his right. A sword was in the executioner's hands.

Pythio was kneeling before "Nemesis," weeping and shaking. "Please," he was murmuring. "Please, please…"

"The holy gods do not suffer liars to live," King Phaedrion said.

It was not true. Taicho, standing, next in line for death, knew many injustices went unanswered. The Kersican League, for example, enslaved countless thousands of Eloesians, reducing them to the state of Elehoi. They pillaged and slaughtered towns that did not submit to them. And yet the Kersican League remained, strong and standing tall, showing little sign of weakness.

Taicho wept and prayed and cursed his life, too short and ending in bitterness. He asked that Father and Mother, and the village elders, would remember him as he wanted them to remember him, as a son who loved them, as a citizen of Lornadion who—despite his many mistakes and disappointments—had left the comfort of his home to fight for a cause greater than himself. He had not shirked the call of duty. He had ventured far across the sea to the motherland, to a place and world he had not known before.

"To Pythio son of Gordios," King Phaedrion said, "I grant you this: one last word. What have you to say?"

"Please… please… don't do this!" Pythio wept.

Around the site of execution, citizens of Kersepoli had gathered to gawk, mostly women. Some had brought their young male children to watch, perhaps to help desensitize them.

Taicho cursed the injustice of it all. He began to weep anew, for Pythio, for Mother and Father, but also for himself. Soon he would join his grandfather and his great uncle in the River of Souls, floating in ignorance and silent sadness, until the day the gods returned to earth.

"Nemesis" stepped before him.

"Three…" the executioner counted.

"No!" Pythio wept.

"Two…!"

"Please," Pythio howled.

"One…!"

"Stop this!" Taicho cried, but the sword fell hard, removing Pythio's head from its body.

"Justice," King Phaedrion said, "from the gods themselves. Praise Tyros. Praise Nemesis."

Hoplites took the body and the head away, disappearing into the darkness.

"Taicho son of Philmedeos," King Phaedrion said, "your justice comes next."

A hoplite roughly grabbed him, dragged him before the executioner and slammed him onto his knees.

"Any last words?" King Phaedrion said. "Speak your peace; then you shall meet your maker."

"I curse you," Taicho said. "And I curse this city, and its League. You are slavedrivers… chattel owners and nothing more. Long live Thénai."

The torchlight illuminated King Phaedrion smile. He raised his hand, and the executioner raised his sword.

"Three…!"

Taicho drew in his breath. Even now, at the moment of death, he thought of Pythio, a young life lost. What a waste… what a tragedy.

"Two…!"

Taicho muttered to his grandfather, peering into the ground below: "Soon, I will see you…"

"One…!"

"*Enough of this*!" Axander's voice rang through the silence of the night. "It is the last night of Yule. The night of mercy. I grant him mercy. Mercy!"

Taicho peered into Axander's eyes. He had not known the hero of Kersepoli to have compassion. He had not known him to show mercy to anyone. But here it was… mercy, on the last night of Yule.

"He is young," Axander said. "He is a fool. Barely more than a child. We send him back on his way, back to Thénai, this very night. Enough blood has been shed. Enough young blood… enough young lives stolen."

"Mercy Axander asks, on this night of Yule," King Phaedrion said, "and mercy I will grant. You are a lucky boy, Taicho son of Philmedeos."

THE HIGH ROAD, ORACLEAN KINGDOM

Three days beyond the town of Laoconia, high into the mountains, the rain had turned to snow, and a bitter wind was blowing. In frozen ponds and streams, amid the swirling white landscape, deer bolted away and the threat of bears was constantly on Herodota's mind. She complained without cease to Geon, complaining that the mission was hopeless, that it was not worth it, that everything she had done and endured this far was without merit.

"Ah!" she cried during an especially large gust, "People live here. People live here. How do they do it?"

The snow was halfway up their boots, which they had exchanged for sandals. Herodota was draped in two winter cloaks, and Geon in one. But nothing could quite take away the chill away, the piercing wind, the driving snow, the hopelessness of the landscape.

Along the road were votive statues, carved in the shape of Maids of Prophecy—young girls in hooded cloaks. This land belonged to the Oracle, and she exerted her control in every way. Her thumb was on everything.

One night, they gathered wood and kindling, and Geon—despite the howling wind and freezing cold—managed to start a fire. In the wonderful warmth of the flame, he took a gander at the wintry world around him, and wondered if they would ever make it to their destination. As he sat there by the fire, the jingling of bells echoed, and he gripped the hilt of his spear.

Amid the darkness, the form of two people on horses emerged, one female, one male, riding quickly down the High Road. They were headed at a trot, ignoring the dreadful weather, silent as they passed by.

"My, my," Herodota said, "Brindos is two days away, and I don't think I can make it."

"We can make it," Geon said. "We *will* make it. We must… for Amara's sake, and for yours."

Herodota remained weak, but her frail human body was not her greatest weakness; no, it was her heart, whose hope had long left, which had only a spark of faith remaining. Geon had to tend it, or it would wink out entirely, and the hope of the world would be gone.

IDRIS VALLEY, THE HIGH ROAD, ORACLEAN KINGDOM

Cadelita was huffing and puffing, straining as she ascended the road.

The snow almost reached her ankles, and occasionally her hoof would slip as she struggled upward.

A storm had entered the valley at dusk, and snow was falling in great white clumps.

The ascent of the High Road was difficult in the spring, when Khloë had last taken it, but traveling to the mountains now, in the height of winter, was a sign of madness, or, in her case, haste.

Theron had announced he would meet her on the first day of spring, and by the holy gods, she intended to be there.

Her journey, long ago, had at last paid off. She had met Theron in his mountain kingdom, and now, many months later, she had changed his heart; he would return to the nation he belonged to, to the League he was a citizen of. He would fight for Thénai's glory; and that glory, the glory of the greatest city in Eloesus, would be written of in history books. Theron's name, and Thénai's, would be exalted for all time.

The air was biting and thin, and all Khloë could do to keep her sanity was to breathe through her nose, and hold her winter cloak as tight as possible while keeping her grasp of the reins.

Khloë knew what they faced: besides bears and wild cats, there were avalanches, frostbite, and innumerable snares. Hektor had allowed them to take the road as soon as the mountain ascent began, because Elena Kaiaphon's men would not be as mad as they; virtually no one took the High Road in winter, let alone in the middle of it.

"Amara help us," Khloë growled as an especially piercing gust of wind chilled her to the bone.

"Amara cannot help us here," Hektor said.

"I thought you believed in the New Gods," Khloë said. "I thought you fought for them."

"I do not fight for the New Gods, or for any abstraction," Hektor said. "I do not really fight against the Old Gods. I fight against the Old *Believers*… because I know what they've done. I know what they're capable of."

Khloë heaved a sigh. Not only was the wintry air bitter, this high up, it was difficult to breathe in the first place. Cadelita stooped down, almost collapsing, and Khloë gasped. At last the mare righted herself and continued her ascent.

In the darkness of the night, she could make out the lights of towns, a warm yellow against the landscape, on the slopes of mountains. They had truly reached the high country, but the Mount of Prophecy remained ten days away, at best, and perhaps more, if the mountain passes had become clogged with snow. They had plentiful food and water, but not enough to last the winter; if they became trapped, they would slowly starve, and, eventually, freeze.

"Amara help us," Khloë said despite Hektor. "Amara help us."

OXFALL ROAD, OUTSIDE BRINDOS

The journey of many days and weeks was about to end.

The sun was shining brightly for once, with hardly a cloud in the sky. On the road, which wound its way across a cliff, the snow had begun to glisten and thaw. The air, cold and crisp, still burned Geon's lungs, but the thought of finally reaching Brindos filled him with joy and expectation.

The road at last took a sharp turn, and the town appeared before them.

Set before a great cliff face, Brindos was tucked into the side of a mountain. Its buildings, all built of wood, had roofs piled with snow, and the chimneys were billowing smoke. On the edge of town, children dressed in furs were throwing a ball.

But Herodota had stopped her walking.

"Geon… I… I am not sure."

Geon stopped just behind her. "We've come this far, Herodota," Geon said.

Yet the greatest test was ahead of her. *What will Hippolyta think of me?* Geon sensed her thoughts. *She will think I am mad!*

Hippolyta, her friend, had been unmarried when she left Brindos, and had been consumed with zeal for the gods. In the time of trouble before Thénai's fall, Hippolyta had fled the city, escaping its tumult and street battles. "Perhaps," Herodota had told him once on this journey, "she sensed disaster coming, long before any of us did."

"Hippolyta," Herodota said aloud. "I am not sure she—"

"We are here," Geon said. "Here, on the roof of the world! Look how far we've come.

"Will you throw it away now? Will you abandon all our hard

work? Surely not!"

It was Herodota who took the first step.

SHRINE OF AMARA, BRINDOS

In the end, it was in the goddess's own shrine where they found Hippolyta.

In the wooden structure, she was kneeling on a rug before the altar, hands raised toward the ceiling, muttering and praying, begging and supplicating.

Figurines of the goddess stood in alcoves throughout the shrine, some lit by the lights of candles. The stone altar was overlaid with a blue cloth.

Hippolyta was a slight woman, slender and short. Her gown was crude and made of cassock. Her hair was a golden brown.

The villagers had pointed them this way; they had not remarked on Geon's appearance. Perhaps, in the brightness of the snow, it was hard to discern a difference.

"Hippolyta," Herodota said. "Friend."

Hippolyta turned and gasped, scrambling backward and catching her balance on the altar. "Gods in heaven, holy, bright… Herodota!"

Hippolyta was a young woman, no more than twenty. Her face was fair, and her eyes were a sky blue. There were no rings on her fingers, no indication of marriage.

Virginity was required for the priesthood of Amara; it was one of the sacred rites, one of the sacred obligations.

"You came for me," Hippolyta said. "All the way from Thénai? For what purpose?

"I left that place of strife behind… but it has come back to me."

Herodota approached the altar. "The Thénai you knew is no more.

"Every priestess has been killed. Southrons slew them. And an abominable statue sits enthroned in the temple… the likeness of a demon, an enemy of mankind."

Hippolyta stood there, slack-jawed, unable to believe.

"I am the only remaining priestess," Herodota said. "I alone know the rites. I alone know the temple ritual. But that can change… with your help."

ARKADION, THEMURIA

Twelve Days Later…

The snow was up to Cadelita's knees, but the descent to Arkadion had been just that… a descent.

Khloë uttered a prayer of praise as the lights of the town appeared.

The town, built on three hills, had grown since Khloë had seen it last, all those years ago.

A ceremonial gate marked the entry to the city, etched of stone in serpentine reliefs. In the town itself, women dressed in blue hoods passed to and fro, marked against the dreary browns and grays of the populace.

The temple was no longer built of wood; facing the city square, hewn of mighty pillars, it was a great stone edifice, dedicated not to Brecko lord of wine but a god Khloë did not recognize; Mira was her name. A solar relief ran along its pediment. Its shingles were brilliant blue.

"Here we are," Hektor said.

Here, in the Oracle's domain, Elena Kaiaphon's dark machinations had no effect, but instead a greater, more powerful woman, one whose motives none could divine, one whose power none could fathom. They had left the certainty of the Eloesian nation behind, and entered a new realm, one of prophecy, mystery and magic.

ARKADION, THEMURIA

It was the first of Alphaios, the first day of spring, but a winter storm had raged just yesterday, further burying Arkadion in snow. Neither the weather nor the sun showed any sign of conforming to the calendar. Perhaps many fathoms below, in the lowlands, the green grass was growing and butterflies were perched on flowers, but here, winter in its real sense would continue.

Khloë had availed herself of Arkadion's hot springs and feasted with abandon in its inns. Well rested, and garbed in a winter cloak, she and Hektor departed on horses, leaving through the free-standing Gate of Prophecy.

The bent peak of the Mount of Prophecy was a dark shadow against the white of the clouds. Khloë's stomach was twisting to knots. She did not know what to expect. Would things be the same? Had her old friend changed? Would he still respect her? He was different now, not just a hero, but a king and who knew what else. In his long absence from Thénai, his power had vastly grown. But would he be the same person? Would he still be Khloë's friend?

~

They rode up switchbacks, through passes clogged with snow. As the day grew late, Khloë thought she heard drums, loud drums whose timbre she did not recognize, and high-pitched laughter coming from high above her. Hektor led the way.

The mountain road took a sharp turn, and Council Overlook appeared before her around the bend, a bit of ground overlooking the Vale of Arkadion far below.

There, standing alone, by himself, was a figure shrouded in shadow. She recognized the lion-skin he wore around his head. She recognized the club in his hands. She recognized his beard, his hands, but above all his dark eyes, glistening in the sunlight.

"Khloë," Theron said. "It is good to see you."

THE POTTER

A FABLE

There once lived a poor potter in the slums of the city.

Without cease, from morning to dusk, he worked the clay with his hands, forming pots and jars and selling them to all, rich and poor.

One day a wicked king took control of the city, and began to oppress his subjects, taxing them beyond their ability to pay. He cleared the house of the potter and the houses of all his neighbors, demolishing them brick by brick to build a great palace for himself.

The potter built out of clay a great giant, with coals for eyes. He prayed and prayed that it would be given life. He offered sacrifices in the city's temple. But the giant remained lifeless, and the king eventually took it and made more bricks for his palace.

The poor suffer, and the rich do what they will.

—Amalchio

BALCONY, ROYAL PALACE, KERSEPOLI

As Axander looked out from the palace balcony, seeing the women and young children in the streets below, he took count of his life, and realized this was not how he thought things would end up, or how what his struggles would come to.

As a young Kersican male, a member of the nobility, he was expected to be a warrior.

He had been taken from his mother, a woman he barely knew, at the tender age of five. Like others his age, he had known nothing except war and battle. Like others his age, he had been taken from his family and placed into a barracks in the wilds. Like the others, he had eaten nothing except black pottage and had drunk nothing except befouled water. He had developed a skill with a spear and shield that rivaled the best of the Chosen.

But there had been a problem, one that had destroyed all his best-laid plans.

He had been left handed. In battle, the Kersican advantage had been marching in lockstep, shield to shield. Everyone Axander had known had been right-handed. There had been no left-handed regiment.

And so, at age thirteen, his battalion commander had cut him free, telling him to return to the city, to learn a trade from the women, to engage in commerce or sail across the seas.

Instead, he had become a brigand. He had waylaid caravans. He had lived for nothing except theft and violence. He had robbed travelers and become immensely wealthy.

That purposelessness had ended years ago, when the Oracle called him; she had made a hero out of him. She had used his strength for her own ends. She had developed him into a great warrior, and then sent him off into the world of Kersican politics, telling him she would call him when she needed him.

That hero's calling had beckoned him a little over a year ago.

Kill Geon. Kill the monster.

He had failed. And so he returned to the politicking and strategy of the Kersican elite.

He cursed his fate as he stood there on the balcony. The weight of failure was on his shoulders.

He was a hero, like Theron or like Phillipidēs. But he had come up short. His mission had ended in disaster, in the deaths of his men and the slaughter of his soldiers.

But worse than anything was failing to answer the calling. He had not done as the Oracle wished.

~

Late at night, King Phaedrion had retired to bed, and Axander returned to his quarters. His room was bare and unornamented as Kersicans liked it: a chamber pot, a cot, a table and a chair, and a pile of unread papers: spy reports and collected information he had paid little attention to. Outside, the moon was shining. It was a full moon, the first moon of the spring, and the wind blowing through Axander's window had a whiff of pollen. The spring did not have as much hope or promise to it as even last year.

For one, the Thenoan League was gaining strength. Each day, thousands of hoplites poured in from the colonies. What the Free and Democratic Armies lacked in skill they more than made up for in sheer numbers. King Phaedrion began to fear they were about to make an offensive. They had retaken Bos, and Free and Democratic armies were marshaling on the border.

Axander uttered a prayer to Tyros lord of war before bed, though Tyros did not pick sides, only delighted in battle.

He had just begun to remove his clothes when there was a knock on the door.

"Excuse me?" he hollered.

"My lord." He recognized the voice of his servant Stratoniko. "I am sorry… I know it is late, but—"

He cracked open the door.

"My lord," Stratoniko said. "I don't know how to put this… you have a visitor. And she… she… uhm, well, let's have you see for yourself."

Axander donned his cloak and buckled his sword to his belt.

He descended to the first floor of the palace, following Stratoniko's footsteps.

When he reached the door, the streets outside were dark, but his visitor was there, holding a lamp in her hands.

He noted her blue hood and knew, beyond a doubt, that this was a Maid of Prophecy, a woman of portent.

"Your Lordship Axander," he said. "I am Noë. Will you have a walk with me?"

Axander's gut dropped. He did not want to face his failure. His failure at slaying Geon already wounded him, already weighed heavily on him. Could he handle the cold remarks of a Maid of Prophecy?

"Very well," Axander said. "Stratoniko? Leave us."

Axander strode out into the night, and Stratoniko shut the door behind them.

~

They spoke of the Oracle; they spoke of wars, in Eloesus and abroad. They spoke of ancient heroes, Phillipidēs and Helemon, Megara and Ionis, and of one she called Pegara. They spoke of the weather, of the warmth of springtime, of the blooming of flowers and the cyclical nature of the seasons which would continue until the gods' return. By the time they were done, they had left the city gate entirely and entered the open fields.

The air was cool, and the moon was shining on the spring grass. On a hill not far from the city walls, someone was waiting for Axander, someone whose towering height and hulking girth he recognized instantly. He had met this creature only once before.

The creature lowered its hood, revealing a bovine, bull-like face, two massive horns on its head, and eyes that twinkled yellow in the moonlight.

"Lord Skauros," Axander said, and dropped to one knee.

He did not know who, or what, this creature was, where it had come from or what its intentions were. Perhaps it was the appellation "Lord" that caused Axander to give deference. Clearly, this Lord Skauros was a high ranking servant of the Oracle, one of her right hands in the mortal realm.

But Skauros did not say anything, only breathed and grunted in the night, giving off fog as he did.

Outside, the crickets were chirping in a constant rhythm. The air was warm, and rich with the scent of flowers. It was hard to feel hopeless on a moonlit spring night, but Axander managed to do just that.

Standing here with the Maid of Prophecy, and with one of the Oracle's highest emissaries, the weight of failure was all about him; all he could think of was the task he had been given, to slay the Monster Geon, and how, when the tide of battle turned against him, he had fled in the most cowardly way imaginable.

Few would understand what it was like to face a creature

like Geon, winged and brilliant, a spear in his hands, a voice like a god, spreading holy terror wherever he went. It had been too much for Axander to withstand; he had been certain of his death, and so he turned, and he fled. He had fled to safety with the captives in hand.

"Rise." Lord Skauro's voice was muffled, as if he struggled to use human speech. "I bring you a message from on high... the Oracle is wrathful with you, Axander, but you may yet redeem yourself."

He would not face Geon. He could not face Geon. To try to kill him was a fool's mission; he was a creature of the sky and clouds, a messenger of the gods. He was too powerful for any in Eloesus.

"Geon—" Axander began.

"No, no," Lord Skauros said. "Do not speak his name.

"Geon is no longer the Oracle's concern. "It is Theron you must kill..."

"Theron? Truly? Theron?" Axander was in disbelief. "The hero of the Southron War?"

"The hero of the Southron War is interfering in matters that are of no concern to him," Lord Skauros said. "He is threatening the fabric of history. He is trying to pluck a thread of destiny from its place."

COUNCIL OVERLOOK, MOUNT OF PROPHECY, THEMURIA

When Khloë first beheld Theron, her reaction was to weep. Crying with abandon, she had first hugged him, full of warmth at seeing her old friend again, at seeing he was all right and unharmed, and knowing that all the troubles of the lowland—the wars raging and the Old Believers rising—no longer mattered. Khloë would fight alongside the one she loved most in the world, the friend she had come to respect and to revere, the hero she adored. "Friend," Khloë said, wrapping him in her embrace. "It is so good to see you. How many years has it been?"

But when she stepped back, Theron was not smiling; he was solemn and somber. "I have come to make things right," Theron said. "I have come to set things as they must be. And it may cost me my life."

"Your life?" Khloë said. "No, no, I will not let that happen to you. No harm will come to you. I won't have it."

Theron took a step back. He motioned, and Hektor turned his head. "We are not alone," Theron announced.

Khloë turned around. A woman was approaching the snow-blown platform, garbed in a white hooded cloak that seemed far too light for the weather. The sun shone brightly on the silk-like fabric that she almost seemed to glow. Her hood covered most of her face.

Theron knelt before her, and Khloë and Hektor followed a moment later. Who was this, Khloë wondered. She had to be important for Theron to show deference, which he never showed for generals and kings.

The woman lowered her hood, revealing white sightless

eyes and pallid skin. Her hair was a dark black. Coiled within her cloak was a snake, whose head emerged near her neck. The snake turned to look at them with its yellow eyes and forked tongue, which it flicked at intervals.

Khloë's insides felt like they turned to jelly. Instantly, she knew who this woman was, the virtual queen of this region, the master of prophecy and magic, the weaver of destiny. This was the Oracle, the high priestess of all Eloesian religion, surpassing even Amara's faithful. No one's word was taken as seriously; no one else was treated with as much reverence. She was Eloesus' heart, the nation's living soul. She had been absent for centuries, but in recent times she had re-emerged, and her temple had been consecrated once more.

"Theron," she said, "you have neglected this land. You have departed it entirely; and look what has become of it."

"I am not proud of what I did," Theron said.

"Lies!" the Oracle shouted. "You are proud of what you did. You are not proud of the nation, as it is now. You are not proud of your city Thénai. She has transformed. She has become something entirely different. Under the rule of Queen Elena, she grows more and more distant from her past. More distant from her ancient gods. More reverent in its honor of Kronos."

Queen Elena… she had spoken those words. Khloë had not misheard her. Had Thénai abandoned democracy entirely? What, then, was the purpose of the Free and Democratic Armies? If spreading Thénai's ideals was no longer its cause, then what did the soldiers fight for? For "Queen" Elena's riches? For fear of "Queen" Elena's wrath?

"Know this," the Oracle said. "Three truths I give you, before you depart.

"There is a queen in Thénai, but soon she will be wed. A new husband she shall take.

"In the streets of Thénai, the poor live in terror, and the rich have accepted her rule."

The rich never wanted to risk anything. They had too much to lose.

"The third truth, Theron, is this," the Oracle intoned, "that Thénai, and her League, will prevail if left alone. The city's glory will reach the gods' holy mount, and surpass it. Thénai shall bring the southrons low, and all will honor her name."

"Some things are more important than victory," Theron said. "Some things are of greater value than power. It would be better for Thénai to crumble than to lose its soul."

The Oracle laughed, a cold, hollow laugh, one which echoed across the snow-blown platform of Council Overlook.

The wind had picked up pace, driving bare the rocky outcrop, revealing the four symbols which marked the four great cities of Thénai: Tharta a lion, Thénai a ram, Korthos a goat, Kersepoli a wolf. The symbols had been etched in time immemorial when the cities had begun their rise to power. Back then, Tharta outshone them all and now the once-great city had fallen into shadow and southron despotism.

"Meet my soldiers in the lowland, Theron, one month from now. I told you the place," the Oracle said. "We shall drive out Elena Kaiaphon together, with all her bandits. And I shall name you king… King, not just of the Mountain and the Lost Islands, but of all Eloesus… Tharta and Thénai and Ten Cities alike."

But Khloë knew her friend, that kingship was not what he desired; no, he desired the peace and safety of his homeland.

"To Septimon Hill we go," Theron answered her. The Oracle turned and left.

~

They departed together, leaving the mountainside and all

its steep drops and travails.

But when they returned to Arkadion in the evening, they did not go west toward Thénai and Septimon Hill, but instead south during the Old Mountain Road.

"Where are we going?" Khloë said.

Theron rode a horse of his own, a mighty white steed with a gray-speckled back.

"The Oracle thinks I am a fool," Theron said. "But I know her intent. She wishes to ambush me in Septimon Hill. To kill me. I am a threat to her machinations. She does not wish to defeat Elena Kaiaphon; instead, she wishes to leave her as a pawn in her hand. And I will not allow it."

"Then where are we going?" Khloë said.

"To Tharta," Theron said. "To the Royal City."

"Why?" Khloë asked.

"I will tell you," Theron said, "in time."

HILLS OUTSIDE KERSEPOLI

"To Septimon Hill?" Axander said, and breathed in the cold night air.

"A trap has been set," Lord Skauros said, "and you will catch your master's prey. You will have aid. And you will complete your mission this time. You will not flee, or you will regret the day you were born."

In some ways, Axander already did. But he had a chance to redeem himself. He had a chance to prove himself to the Oracle, the woman who had granted him a new life and a purpose. He swore to the holy gods, to the Kersican League, and to his ancestors, he would carry out the act. He would plunge his sword through Theron's heart, and the Hero of the Southron War would fall. Then Axander's name would be remembered like Phillipidēs, even if it earned the people's hatred; he would join the ranks of Ionis and Helēmon, and tales would be told of him long after he was dead.

SPEAR OF THE SEAS, HARBOR, THÉNAI

The air was warm, and the smell of dead fish was omnipresent, when Taicho's ship washed ashore.

He had not been able to do much on the ship, so grieved and haunted he had been by Pythio's death. The young man had been a liar, a deceiver, but only out of self-preservation. He wondered if there was more to that Pythio than he had let on, if there was a secret he had yet held within, one which would now never come to the surface. The executioner's stroke had nearly ended Taicho's life, and now, for better or worse, he intended to make the most of the life he had been given, to right the wrongs he had committed, to join the Free and Democratic Armies without a hint of cowardice.

Taicho stepped off the ship.

It had not been that long since he arrived in Thénai for the first time as a new recruit, but there was something different, something he couldn't place… was it in the air? A trick of the light? Though sailors and merchants were shouting and hollering, unloading their ships with fresh goods, and commerce was buzzing, a whiff of danger hung over everything… a spirit of disaster.

~

The streets through the Long Walls were overloaded with carts bringing cargoes into the city proper. In the distance, Taicho heard laughter and music. Perhaps, it was all in his head, but there was something in the air he felt, an air of joy before a great fall.

By the time he passed through the gates and entered the city proper, the feeling had vanished entirely.

On the side of the road, a woman in a scarlet gown was dancing with blue streamers in her hands, twisting this way and then that, and around her young men had stopped to gawk. In another place, a southron man in a turban had a monkey in a cage which he had trained to dance. Taicho had never seen such revelry and laughter; Thénai had been a somber place when he left. Now, the city was rising anew from the ashes of destruction.

The smells of spices and cooked food wafted in from City Square, and each inch of the street was packed. The cacophony, a thousand different sounds, shouts, grating wheels, barking dogs, and idle chatter, was omnipresent. Thénai was different, yes, in a good way, but as the street opened up into City Square, that familiar unsettled feeling crept over Taicho, the worry that not all was as it seemed. He could not put a finger on it. He looked up to the High City, where the temple was, and the House of the Archon. To re-register for the Free and Democratic Armies, he would have to venture there. He would make an account of what he did; he would ask the judge for another chance.

~

People were walking up and down from the High City, but in less number than the packed city streets below. The air was crisp and cool; spring was here, and the sweltering days of summer remained far off. The war season had begun in earnest, and no doubt, far afield from Thénai, armies—both Free and Democratic and Kersican—were preparing for battle. Taicho would rejoin them; he would reclaim his honor. He would fight, and face his fears this time. He did not have Pythio to turn and run, to encourage him in the way of cowardice, and yet he had to remind himself—their acts of cowardice had saved their lives.

Pythio. He still thought about him, every day, a sad young

man, a lost soul, who had answered the call of the motherland. He had tried to preserve his life, first in the Siege of Bos and then in Kersepoli's royal palace. In the end, death had found him, dragging him down into the underworld, into the River of Souls. He would not enter the Fields of Paradise like the heroes, the Strategoi and the great men did. He was not a prince, like he had said. He prayed as he walked, to the holy gods, for the family Pythio left behind, which endured in the world of the living. Pythio had never spoken of them. Pythio had not spoken much. Perhaps, back in his home in Khazidea, they wondered what happened to their son.

Taicho turned up the ramp to the High City. He would stand before a military judge; he would make an accounting of his failures, of his cowardice. He would return home to Lornadion, either in honor, or bearing shield and spear on a bier.

~

Of all things on the mostly-empty High City, it was the temple that seemed to have changed.

The doors were open, but the sanctuary was completely dark, without candle or torch. The roof had been repainted, and the shingles were now a dull green instead of bright red. The frieze which once ran along the pediment had been etched away, leaving a hollow space. Nonetheless, he offered a prayer to Amara in its direction, that the military judge would accept his service.

~

The law courts were almost completely empty. In one corner, a man and a woman were arguing before a red-garbed judge. In another, a man garbed in black was shouting at a judge; perhaps he had not gotten what he wanted.

But the dais where the military judge once presided was empty.

A man in a black robe was approaching. He had dark eyes and brown hair. He wore, over his head, a crown studded with crescent moons.

Taicho did not know what to say; he had never seen such attire before.

As the man walked, a pair of scorpions skittered away in the direction of the temple.

"What are you doing here, commoner?" the man said.

"I— I— I'm sorry, my good man, I—"

"That is 'my lord' to you. Lord Lysander! Second only to Queen Elena! What are you doing here? Explain yourself!"

His contempt was palpable. The phrase "commoner" had not been used before, not when Taicho was here last. The phrase was largely relegated to southron speech. In Thénai, and the democracies it inspired, all people were meant to be equal in the eyes of the law, with none above or below it. In practice it had been not always that way, but the use of the word "commoner" was striking.

So striking, it was, that he did not know quite how to answer, and fumbled with his words.

"A presumptuous commoner was here last week," Lysander said, "making demands and refusing to leave. He has since vanished. I hope that is not your fate.

"If you wish to live, make a petition to Queen Elena and perhaps she shall grant you an audience in the High City. Until then, depart!"

Taicho, not knowing what else to do, turned and half-walked, half-ran away, away from the High City and its judges, away from the House of the Archon and away from the lonely temple which sat in gloom.

When he returned to the City Square, it was near dusk, and most merchants had packed up their stalls and left. A dog howled. Night would be here soon, and Taicho—with only a few *thalon* to call his own—supposed he would sleep in the streets. He could not spend all his money on creature comforts. In truth, he had only enough to buy food for a day and nothing else. He had expected to join the army quickly, and return to his meager rations while on the march.

In the shadows of the waning sunlight, he realized the House of Assembly where the demiarchs passed laws was no longer there, replaced with a pit of scorched stone and scattered rubble. Had this "Queen" Elena, or whatever she called herself, not only abolished democracy but also destroyed the memory of it? Were all those happy, smiling faces in Thénai's streets accepting of her tyranny?

As the sun began to sink beneath the horizon, he recalled the old stories he'd been told, of Nix, sitting enthroned, the queen of mystery, the lady of magic and the night. He recalled that the barking of dogs heralded her arrival, that She of the Silvered Door, who had one foot in the underworld and in the other in the realm of the living, was lurking in the horizon. He shuddered at the thought of it, at the scary stories told by the fire. He knew they were untrue, but here he was, penniless and unable to survive. If he wanted to return to Lornadion, he couldn't. No ship would take him out of the charity of sailors' hearts.

But that, he realized, was exactly what he had to do.

He fought for the Free and Democratic Armies, not a tyrant queen. He fought for freedom, for liberty and democracy, not a woman who called citizens "commoners."

The sun set in the west, and west was where he would go. West was where his home was.

He would find a way to get there, one way or the other. He

would not fight at the behest of a queen.

THE OLD MOUNTAIN ROAD

On the slopes leading to the mainland, Khloë, Hektor and Theron often had to climb downwards. The drops, at times, were steep and perilous. It had rained the past three nights, and the snow had all but washed away. They were drawing near the border of the high country. Soon they would be in the realm of Tharta, the Royal City which had retreated from the nation's affairs and refused to pick sides in Eloesus' squabbles.

That evening, as the sun shone, Hektor built a fire, a comfort which the trio had not enjoyed in a long time. With twigs and branches, dry logs and kindling, Hektor propped up the wood like a master, and soon it was raging in flame and warmth.

Questions had percolated in Khloë's mind, of where had Theron had been all these years—which he refused to talk about—of how he knew what he did about Elena Kaiaphon, of how he planned to defeat her… but above all, she wondered why they were headed to Tharta, the Royal City.

In better days, during the start of the Southron War, Tharta had refused to lift a finger for the other cities. She had not joined the now long-dead alliance between Kersepoli and Thénai; no, she had looked south, and tried to fuse herself with the southron empire. Why, then, at this dark moment, at this point of hopelessness, would Theron look to Tharta? Why would they go there? Theron remained tight lipped; he refused to say. He refused to inform even his greatest friend, Khloë, who loved him as much as her own self.

Amid the crackling flame, she tried once more: "Theron," she said, "we are going to Tharta. Why?"

"At one time, Tharta was the heart of Eloesus, her anchor,"

Theron said. "It was Tharta where Phillipidēs came from."

Theron was giving Khloë a history lesson as if she did not know. Despite their closeness and their love, it seemed he still viewed her as an outsider, an amazon and not an Eloesian. Of course, she knew the stories of Phillipidēs. Of course, she knew where the greatest hero in Eloesian history came from. Of course, she knew that Tharta was once the greatest city in Eloesus, but she also knew that it was great no longer.

"Is that why we are going?" Khloë said. Her tone was slightly dismissive, and she wondered if she had provoked him to wrath.

Instead, he smiled and laughed. "I have a plan, Khloë. I always have a plan," Theron said. "We are going to free Eloesus, Khloë. We are going to destroy the abomination in the temple. And we are going to kill every single one of Kronos' 'priests.'"

That was what concerned him, not the Thenoan League or the Kersican League, only the temple and what lay within.

It was hard for Khloë to shift focus. Her heart was still set against the Kersicans and their slavery, their autocracy and tyranny. She still felt loyal, above all, to the League she had served for so long.

And yet, she realized, as Theron said, that there were greater things than power, more important things: human souls.

Still she resisted. She had spent all these years, all this countless effort, in service to the military league which Thénai presided over. That had been her life's work. Could she turn back now? Could she threaten its foundations, plunge it into chaos, for the sake of an abstraction, a goddess who never listened when her followers prayed, a goddess incapable or unwilling to save her city when it was first destroyed? Could Kronos, another abstraction, be any worse than that?

Theron's smile had vanished, and his eyes were gleaming in

the firelight. It was as if he had read her mind.

"Khloë," he said, "when we reach the lowland, we will still be in danger. We must never separate."

Khloë glanced at Hektor. "And Hektor—" she began.

"Hektor is leaving us when we reach the Sun King's Road," Theron said. "He is headed toward Thénai to prepare for the battle."

"The Battle." It seemed ominous, final, and the way he spoke it, it was as if the gods would return to earth on that day, to set all things right, to deliver justice. And yet, Khloë would join that very battle, risking the Thenoan League on Amara's behalf. She was still reluctant… Thénai's institutions, its safety and security, would all crumble.

It is Elena Kaiaphon's fault, not mine. The thought was little comfort to her. Elena Kaiaphon had stolen Thénai from under its feet; she had declared herself queen, but it was not only her Khloë would be fighting against. No doubt many commanders, many Strategoi and noblemen, remained loyal to the Thenoan League even after the change of leadership. They would resist Theron's attack as much as anyone else. She would have to spill blood… of friends, of common citizens, of Thenoan patriots.

Say what you would about Old Believers, they were full of zeal and wrath, and they would die before allowing Theron to destroy their abominable statue. Total war would be required… for Amara's sake. For an abstraction. So far from heaven, that is what she seemed. That is how all the gods seemed.

Khloë wondered why Theron wanted her company, why he did not want to do this alone. All this blood would be on her hands… for Amara's cause, yes, but blood would be on her hands.

"To Tharta we go," Khloë said above the raging flames. "To Tharta. Theron, I would follow you anywhere… even to Dys. Even to the edge of the world."

CITY SQUARE, THÉNAI

The sun had set, and the moon had emerged. Taicho found a dark spot in the shadow of a building, and pulled his cloak over himself like a blanket.

He heard idlers in the City Square, talking in low tones.

"Mount Kronos!" the merchant said, "I never saw so much fire and smoke. I do not think the farmers in the valley will ever return."

"Was it worse than before?" said his companion, a woman.

"The worst eruption anyone has ever seen…"

Eventually, their voices faded away as they walked off, dark shadows against a dark canvas.

Though the City Square was mostly empty, and the darkness almost complete, torches were burning along the perimeter, reflecting on the bronze statues of hoplites.

A rift had opened up partway through City Square, and Taicho recalled the earthquake that had struck not long ago. Not all of it had been repaired. Things were different, yes, but it was more than the torches, more than the broken stone, more than the destroyed House of Assembly. It was something he couldn't put his finger on, something he couldn't explain, something that would cause others to think he was crazy if he voiced it.

"Hey! You, there," a woman said. She was approaching.

She was gaunt and tall, and as she drew near, the torchlight reflected on her thigh-high skirt, her black brassiere, and her dark sandals. Her hair was a dark blonde, and her eyes a pale blue. Across her face were jagged scars, perhaps venereal in nature. Taicho found himself crawling away.

"You look lonely over there," the woman continued. "It's cold out. Don't you want some company?"

"No," Taicho found himself muttering. "No, no. No thank

you."

He had begun to creep away from her.

"Are you scared? Don't be scared," she said. "Don't be afraid of what's down here in City Square… be afraid of what's up there."

She was pointing to the High City, which was shrouded in darkness, without illumination.

The prostitute kept walking toward him and he scrambled to his feet, running away from her. He was not safe. He would not be safe, not as long as he stayed in the city. He had to get on a ship, and leave, as soon as he could, as swiftly as his sandals could take him.

He turned down a darkened street and tripped, falling face-down. With bruised knees he scrambled to his feet, and there, in the light of the moon, two eyes were gleaming.

An assortment of beggars were sleeping on this street corner; Taicho had tripped on one of their legs, an old man with a white beard. He was wrapped in a blanket and fleas were buzzing around it.

In better times, Taicho would be disgusted. Now he was one of them.

There were about a dozen in total, huddled together in blankets, men, women, young and old, including five children. These were the city's refuse. They were like Taicho, without hope or purpose in the world. Yet they were worse off; they did not have a mother and a father eagerly awaiting their return. They did not have a warm bed waiting for them on the other side of the world, in Lornadion.

"I am sorry," Taicho said. "I am sorry, my good man."

The old man mumbled something indistinguishable.

"You are not from around here." The woman was talking. Her hair was brown and tangled, and her five children were sleeping next to her in various positions. "You should be careful. You should not sleep alone. Not in this city, not anymore. Do you have children? Keep them near you! You are a foreigner, and you do not understand…"

Taicho was not inclined to believe this homeless woman, who could be suffering from delusions.

"There are people disappearing! Women, children…. you could be next," the woman continued. "You are not safe! Not safe!"

At the sound of her hysterical words, the old man tried babbling again, but made no sense.

The stench of these people was overpowering. No doubt they had not bathed in months.

"Queen Elena is not a good woman," she said, whispering, speaking in hushed tones as if she feared the night birds would go tell her. "You do not understand… you are a foreigner…"

One of her children began to weep and flail. The old man began to scream.

Taicho turned and fled into the night.

The street lamps offered little illumination, and as Taicho ran down the road, he noted the complete absence of people. The words of the homeless woman echoed in his mind and he wondered if she might just be right, if the new government of Thénai was truly killing its own citizens. But why, and how? Why would they slay their own citizens? What could a government possibly gain from that? No doubt she was mad, but she had clutched her children tight as if she truly believed it.

~

In the morning, he awoke slumped under a rooftop. The night had been so manic and frightful he at first didn't realize where he was. But gulls were soaring overhead, and the smell of fish was omnipresent, the sounds of carriages rattling on the road was deafening, and the cacaphony of sailors shouting formed an overwhelming noise.

He had taken shelter in the harbor. He had become convinced, in the dim light of the street lamps, that someone had been following him. Now, in the light of day, it seemed silly. He remembered shadows, cast in the dim illumination. It had all been a mistake, a trick of the light. He laughed in the light of dawn. But he was hungry, very hungry. The few *thalon* he had in his possession might buy him a fish, and here, in the harbor, fishermen who'd left before dawn were just now returning.

But hungry as he may be, he had one goal: to leave this place, to go back home, to face whatever justice Lornadion had for a deserter. He had to be prudent. He had to keep his money; he had to save, hard as it may be, or else he'd never leave Thénai. He would never leave this place.

In the sea, the sailing season had begun in earnest, and now ships of all sizes were headed from port to port throughout the sea. Each one of them might get him to Dys, if he tried. He did not have the money, but he could beg.

~

He went from ship to ship inquiring. One ship was headed to Khazidea, another to Bregantion, one to "Sanctum," wherever that was. It was late in the morning when he found a departing ship headed his way, to the "nine Isles and Dys."

The sailor was a large, red faced man dressed in white. His sailors were loading amphorae by the cart into the hull of the ship.

His name, Taicho soon learned, was Nikolao, and he was a seasoned sailor, having gone to every known port in the sea in his long career.

"My lord," Taicho used a title reserved for royals. "I will do anything... anything! If you take me home, to Dys. You may drop me anywhere you'd like. I'll work as hard as you want, on anything at all."

Nikolao smiled. "You are young," he said. "Hot-headed. You should join the army. When you return from your tour, you'll have enough money to travel with me. Perhaps, if you plunder a city, then you can buy your own ship and a crew of your own!"

"I have seven *thalon*," Taicho said. "Seven *thalon*. That's all. But I will be a hard worker."

"If I offered journeys to every poor beggar," Nikolao said, "I would have a full deck. Come back when you are a rich man, young Taicho. I believe in you."

Taicho turned in agony, and walked away, out of the harbor, and eventually, through the Long Walls, and into the city itself.

~

He spent every last coin he had in City Square. He ate a loaf of sweetbread and bought a hunk of cured meat. He drank the tangy juice of a pomegranate; and then he was penniless, poor and destitute.

The sun had reached its highest point in the sky, casting long shadows, when Taicho had retreated to City Square's perimeter, cursing what he had done. He had acted impulsively, prizing his stomach above all else, and now look at him. Look at what had happened. Tears formed in his eyes as he watched the prosperity and commerce all around him.

He began to question himself, and everything he had done. Perhaps, he *would* have to fight for a cause he did not believe in. Perhaps, he'd grow hungry enough he would fight for Queen Elena, not for the Free and Democratic Armies but for the whim of a woman who called her people "commoners."

A horn blew, loud and piercing like a trumpet, and the merchants and buyers paused their commerce. In an instant, City Square was silent and still. They were looking up, toward the ramp from the High City, and Taicho followed their gazes.

Up above him, a procession was headed downward into the city streets, a hundred black garbed men and women, and in the center a woman on a litter. In the front and back of them were battalions of hoplites, perhaps numbering five hundred in total. They held spears and shields in their hands, and the horsehair crests of their helmets were bright blue. At the head of them was a commander whose armor was embossed in gold; he blew his horn again.

A few of the idlers in City Square turned and ran in fear; others stood still in anticipation.

It was clear: the "Queen" of the Thenoan League was approaching them.

~

At the west-facing edge of Thénai was a stone lectern on a raised podium. The people of City Square gathered around it, and Taicho, after a moment of hesitation, followed. Politicians gathered here to give their speeches, and it was clear the "queen" was preparing to speak to them.

What use was a lectern, now, and a podium, when there were no longer candidates seeking office? The House of Assembly lay totally in rubble, and monarchy had replaced Thénai's remarkable way of government. There was no need to appease the masses, no need to serve the people or give any care for their needs. What use, then, was speech? What use, then, was a podium?

Taicho remembered well when Lornadion had sworn allegiance to the Thenoan League, and villagers partook in a sacrificial offering to Thénai's civic gods. He had been seven years old. Not long afterward, teachers had come to instruct the children of Lornadion, of what Thénai was, what she represented and her method of government. Those teachers, sent to Lornadion, on the western edge of the world, had taught of Thénai's founding, how, at the end of the Archaic Age, she overthrew her tyrant king, and the radical leader Ansolon and his wife Hordo proclaimed "the people would rule." The disorderly nature of popular vote eventually gave way to the form of democracy the world knew today… or at least, the form that once existed, before Queen Elena.

Taicho looked upon the "queen" with resentment as she approached the stage.

She appeared old, and used a cane as she walked. It was as if she had wilted away. Still, she raised herself to the lectern. "Citizens! Countrymen! Patriots!" the so-called queen said. "I have come to announce two things: one great, one greater.

"King Leonaras of Kersepoli has been slain on the field of battle. He has fallen, and the town of Phalkis with it. The Elehoi have been freed! They are no longer slaves! And the Kersican Armies have begun to falter! Victory is upon us! Sweet victory, in our lord's name!"

The crowd gathered around the lectern had begun to cheer.

Who was this "lord?" Thénai served a lady, Amara Queen of Battle, not a lord. What did the so-called Queen Elena mean?

"And secondly, you know our kingdom has long been without a king!" Elena said. "No longer. I shall continue to rule, but know that Pereon of Phos shall be my consort!"

The cheering was slightly less. Victory was much more reinvigorating to the spirits, and few cared about Elena or her new husband.

"One more thing have I to say!" Elena said. "In the ruins of the House of Assembly, something new shall be built, something consequential. And Thenoans shall build it! By Thenoan hands, a new shrine shall rise. By Thenoan hands, a new victory will be had.

"No longer will Tharta be the hegemon of Eloesus. No longer will the Royal City loom large in the hearts and minds of our people, but instead the Free and Democratic one, the birthplace of liberty!"

The cheering had become deafening, now. But her words rang false. How could she claim liberty, freedom, and democracy when she ruled as a queen? She couldn't.

Taicho alone did not clap. But now his thoughts turned to Tharta. The Royal City still loomed large in his heart; the Thartans had founded his hometown, Lornadion, as a colony in time immemorial.

Tharta… the Royal City. The nation of Eloesus had been divided in half, Thénai on one side and Kersepoli on the other. No one talked about Eloesus' most ancient city, not anymore.

ROYAL THARTAN ROAD, THARTICA

It had now been weeks since Hektor departed; when they reached the lowlands, he had left northward for Thénai, brave soul that he was. He was preparing for battle, but in all this time, Theron—walking beside Khloë—had not told her why they were going to Tharta, why they were headed toward a city that had shrunk in power, prestige and importance. He would not tell her, no matter how much she asked.

Now they rode alone, down a sparsely populated thoroughfare.

On either side of the bright white road were funeral monuments: tombs, markers and mausoleums crammed together in various shades of white, gray and yellow. It was remarkable to Khloë, as she rode onward, just how many monuments there were, how many dead people had longed to be remembered. How many countless people, how many millions, were now in the underworld, living in the depths of the earth, in inky darkness, without knowledge or hope? The dead of ancient Tharta had desired for the living to consider them. Khloë remembered Arkelaios' ancient epic, how what the hero Phillipidēs wanted above all else was imperishable fame, a good name to be remembered. He was no different from these departed souls: soldiers and merchants, potters, blacksmiths and husbandmen, craftsmen and artisans, who spent vast sums to be buried on the side of the road. Now, their names and their lives were etched in stone… they were eternal.

If Theron attracted little attention, it was because the sparsity of travelers on the road. Khloë relished in the remembrance that Elena Kaiaphon had no power here. She was safe, when they camped among the graves. She was safe, when she traveled the

Royal Thartan Road. The wars of greater Eloesus had nothing to do with Tharta, and here, in Eloesus' most ancient region, the squabbles were far away and remote, and did not come to mind.

Yet this was also a place of gloom, and travelers along the Royal Thartan Road seemed somber, never laughing and smiling. Perhaps, it was the funerary monuments crammed alongside the road. Death was never far from one's thoughts.

One evening, three days from the Royal City, Theron stopped off the side of the road. They tied their horses to posts, and Theron sent Khloë off to gather wood.

In the tombs, she dallied.

THINDOS, SON OF THINDOS, one tombstone read, FISHMONGER. HUSBAND. FRIEND. MAY THE LIVING REMEMBER ME.

Others were more ancient, in Archaic Eloesian and in other languages which Khloë did not recognize. Some had no writing at all, only white stone posts hammered into the ground, marking the place of burial.

As Khloë witnessed so much death, a heaviness began to settle over her heart. Wasn't it where they were all headed? The underworld was everyone's destination, the darkness of the pit, for anyone who had been born or would be born. Only the great entered the Fields of Paradise. The River of Souls, encircling the island of the underworld, was the destination of the small. That was what tradition taught, in Eloesus, and in Amazonia, from whence Eloesians plucked their religion.

When she returned, it was dark, and the moon had arisen, white and bright, a waning crescent. They were on the cusp of summer. Further afield, in Thénai, the fighting season was raging, and no doubt the nation was ripping itself apart. Khloë despaired at the thought. And she despaired at what she meant to do. They would have to attack Thénai, her city, to destroy the abominable statue and its abominable priests. Khloë did not know how Theron intended to overcome the Free and Democratic Armies, but she knew his wisdom and strength, and that he would find a way.

Together, they fashioned the fire. Theron struck a spark with flint and tinder, and like clockwork, it began to burn.

As she peered into his eyes in the fire, she noted they were full of thought.

He had kept so much to himself over these past months. So much had been left unsaid, and Khloë still—after all this time—had not been told the purpose of this journey.

Not one for giving up pointless pursuits, she asked again, "Theron. I have gone so long without knowing. Tell me! Why are we going to the Royal City? Why are we going to Tharta?"

"Do you know," Theron said softly, almost mumbling, "why the Oracle is intent on killing me? Do you know why she has tried to kill me before?"

Khloë looked down, peering into the fire and its red-hot coals, staying silent for a few moments.

The Oracle was a prophetess and a seer who had reigned in her truth long before humans arrived. She had sat on her holy mount long before humans came to Eloesus. She was there when amazons lived in harmony in their homeland. She had been a fixture of amazonian life; the first Oracle, it was said, had been a blind amazon girl, a snake charmer from the amazon capital of Rhegia. Rhegia was gone, and so was its memory, but the Oracle remained, consumed with zeal.

"No," Khloë said. "I do not know why the Oracle would want to kill you. Why would the Oracle kill a hero she raised?"

"I began to see things," Theron said. "I began to notice things in the wider world. I began to see how one thing would lead to another, how everything leads to something in this culmination we call history.

"It's called destiny. When the wind of destiny blows, the Oracle can feel it. I began to feel it too.

"And now, Khloë, I see the way things are headed. They are headed to a bad place. We are going to Tharta, Khloë, to change the course of history…

"We are going to take a thread out of destiny's fabric. To change the way things are. To alter destiny… to seize hold of the world, and history, and blow the wind off course."

SEPTIMON HILL, THENOA

The night was dark and cloudless.

Axander was marching, following Lord Skauros and Noë as he had since the very beginning.

Lord Skauros was bearing a great torch that served as a beacon in the blackness.

They were drawing near their destination; Axander could sense it in his bones. A pall had settled over him, over everything. His gut had twisted into knots. He was not often afraid, but dread was building in his heart, dread he could not explain. The night was too dark; it was almost pitch black, and against the silence of the night something was rising from far away, a noise not of sound, but of mind. Something was watching him. He, and Lord Skauros, and Noë, were not alone.

When the drums began, Axander's hand went to his sword, but he stopped himself. Lord Skauros turned, yellow eyes twinkling, and began to laugh, a deep, hollow sound.

Lights appeared in quick succession, a dozen, then a hundred, illuminating a tall hill.

Not far away was the sea, and the waves were gently rolling to shore. The air smelled of pollen and freshness. It was wonderfully cool, but all was not well.

A hundred people, perhaps, were gathered on the hill, on its summit and around its base. But who stood at its apex was what he dreaded above all: the Oracle, garbed in a snow-white dress. Even from far away, Axander could feel her eyes staring at him, examining him, measuring up his worth. She knew everything, past, present, and future. Through her dark whispers, she beguiled kings and great men, and manipulated the course of history. She was prophecy embodied.

He remembered the first time he had been called.

He had been a brigand. Axander, the scion of a noble family, had been left handed, unable to join the army or become a member of the Chosen like he'd dreamed. Instead, he had waylaid caravans in the foothills of the Sky Mountains, harassing Thenoan merchants as they passed along the way. In his delusion, he had thought of the robberies as a patriotic duty, a service to the People and the City of Kersepoli. By robbing the citizens of its rival, he had puffed up grand notions of what he was doing, and considered it noble.

But one evening not long ago, a Maid of Prophecy had approached the bandit camp. "Axander, son of Philippos," she had said, "I bear a message from the Oracle on her holy mount. She has chosen you."

He had tried, in vain, to answer her hero's calling. But he had failed; the monster Geon had slipped from his grasp. Now, a new mission was at hand: to slay not a monster of the celestial realm, but instead to kill Eloesus' national hero, a man who was revered not just in his hometown of Thénai but also in Korthos, Kersepoli and the wider world. Axander had no choice but to try. He had failed once; he would not fail again. He would slay Theron, the hero of the Southron War, or he would die trying.

Why the Oracle had changed her mind, Axander had no idea. But she had apparently lost interest in Geon. She was as capricious as the gods in heaven; her mind changed like the wind. She was slippery and cunning, but in all her decisions, Axander was convinced there was a master plan.

With no small bit of hesitation, Axander approached Septimon Hill. The roaring of the sea became audible, and it was comforting in its constant rush. But the people standing around the Oracle frightened him; they were darkly-garbed, but there eyes were dark too, almost black, and the torches' glint was almost swallowed up beside him.

Axander walked off toward the hill, with Skauros just behind.

The black-garbed men and women bearing torches were smiling. At the Oracle's side was a woman, older than the rest, with long brown hair visible inside her hood. On the other side of them was a tall man, garbed in a dark cloak, his features hidden by a hood. A great sword of iron was clipped to his side.

Smiling brightly was the Oracle. Her snake was wrapped around her leg, coiled around her torso and peering over her shoulder. When the snake's yellow eyes met Axanders', he sensed a soul within them and not an animal. He felt naked before the snake's gaze, as if it saw everything about him, his insecurities, his future and his past, his weaknesses, his dark secrets. Yet he could not look away from those yellow eyes. It was as if a spell had been cast on him

"Axander," the Oracle's voice jolted him away from the gaze. Her eyes were no less spellbinding.

"We have been betrayed," the Oracle continued.

SEPTIMON HILL, THENOA

The night was deep, and cicadas were chirping. The crickets formed a deafening rhythm. Summer was almost at the door.

Axander knelt before his master, the Oracle. The foreboding pall was almost overwhelming now. He sensed there was more to this hill than he knew, a long and storied history, much of it good but most of it bad. He sensed that many had spent time here, on nights just like this one, and many lives had been lost as well. He sensed whatever the history of Septimon Hill was, he did not want to know it.

In the light of the torches, he noted an altar had been built, crudely, of stone.

"We have been betrayed," the Oracle repeated herself. "I told Theron to meet us here, but he is too clever for us. He has turned south. To Tharta. To the Royal City which now stands condemned by Eloesus and the gods alike. Why he has gone, it is not for you to know."

Perhaps, the Oracle herself did not know. It was hard to believe that she did not know everything. When she stared at Axander, it seemed as if she was peering into deep waters, into the depths of his soul.

"When he left with the centaur—"

Were centaurs not creatures of myth?

"—I thought I had rid of him. I thought he had left Eloesus altogether. I thought he would become a great king far away… found a kingdom in the mountains.

"But he has returned, my Axander. Theron has returned! He has come back to Eloesus, to meddle in affairs that are not his.

"He has turned against his city Thénai. He no longer cares for his city, or for Eloesus, only grand notions of humanity. He is a fool, Axander, though he does not know it! He does not know what he is dealing with. He does not know what he contends with. He is awakening something he cannot control, something that will destroy him.

"He will burn Thénai if he must."

Axander was a Kersican, and a proud one. The Oracle was making Theron sound like an ally.

The Oracle was silent for a while, and the wind was rustling through the grass. In the light of the torches, it dawned on him: the woman, standing next to Oracle, was the one who called herself "Queen," the one who had destroyed Eloesian democracy.

Was Axander's loyalty no longer to Kersica above all?

Would his loyalty to her truly surpass his own people, his own city, his own home?

He had bent a knee to the Mount of Prophecy and the woman who lived upon it. But seeing Queen Elena, his mortal enemy, the foe of the Kersican League, he began to waver, to question everything he had done.

"Theron must die," said the woman he believed was Queen Elena. "And once he is dead, Axander, we will make a treaty with the Kersican League. We will be at peace. And we will install *you* as king."

Queen Elena had great delusions of her own power. That much was clear. The tide had begun to turn, but the Thenoans were not on the verge of victory, not yet. King Leonaras had been slain in Phalkis, stabbed in the heart on the field of battle, but King Phaedrion still reigned in Kersepoli. Korthos had begun to bristle under Kersican control, but it had not outright rebelled or overthrown its allegiance. Tharta had begun to turn against the Kersicans, but it remained neutral for now. Queen Elena was no kingmaker, at least, not yet.

Behind him, the great footsteps of Lord Skauros echoed, grinding the earth under his hooves.

Queen Elena screamed, and her hooded husband backed away. "What is this?" she cried. From her side she drew a dagger. "Back away, monster!"

"He is no monster," the Oracle said, "he is Lord Skauros. He is an avatar of time. He is the last of his people. And he is my ally… and yours."

Lord Skauros knelt before her.

Queen Elena put her dagger back in its sheath, but looked no less disturbed.

"What now, my lady?" Axander said.

"Now, we prepare," the Oracle said. "We go to Thénai. We make ready for what is coming."

Axander had indeed made a decision. His loyalty was not to the Kersican Army, who rejected him, but instead to the Oracle, who had given him a purpose. It was her, only, who he would serve.

CITY SQUARE, THÉNAI

For five *thalon* a day, for the past four weeks, Taicho had worked ceaselessly.

He had cleared away the debris, brick by brick, from the House of Assembly. But he was no richer than when he began.

They were building, now, a Royal Assembly, one which would serve the purposes of Queen Elena and her husband. The construction would begin in the morning.

At times, Taicho despaired. The promise of returning home on a ship was as far away as ever. He had not managed to save a single coin.

The workman blew a trumpet, signaling the day's work was done.

Taicho, covered in sweat and grime, turned to leave. He had been put up in a ramshackle building on the edge of town. He spent every last bit of his meager money on food, but at least he had a roof over his head, and a cot that he could sleep on. That, he supposed, was the best he could hope for.

He began to question whether he would ever leave Thénai, or if he would be stuck in this cycle of poverty forever, waking up at dawn, and working until sundown.

His friends from the worksite were calling after him. Perhaps, they intended on drinking at one of Thénai's many taverns. But he turned and waved them off. He did not want to drink, not tonight, or do anything, really. The burden of these past weeks, and the fading dream of returning home, had begun to weigh on him.

When he returned to his small room in the corner of the house, it was dark, and a fire was burning in the hearth. Other impoverished laborers, who shared this dwelling place, had gathered there among the flames. But Taicho did not follow them.

He was weary, in his body and his bones, and he was weary, in mind and soul. He wanted nothing less than the company of others.

Still slightly hungry, he nonetheless hopped in his cot. In the darkness, he tugged his blanket tight and, eventually, drifted off, into the world of sleep.

~

He dreamed that night, of winter storms, and a great wind tossing up the sea. Out of the waves, against the steely sky, he saw a dark shape rising, as large as a city, so large that as it emerged the waters began to swirl around it. He could not see the features of the beast, but he knew it was staring at him. Compared to the beast, he was a speck of sand on the seashore.

The dream faded away, and in its place came another, none less dreadful.

He was back in the City Square of Kersepoli. It was night, as dark a night as Taicho had ever seen.

He was standing there alone, and amid the dim torchlight, someone was approaching.

It was Pythio, without his head. On his tattooed chest, his egret necklace remained, the one he had stolen from a rich man.

"Why were you spared?"

How was Pythio talking without a head?

"Why did Axander let me die and not you? Why was he only merciful to you?"

~

The morning light awoke Taicho. The summer air was warm, but he had never felt so cold, not even in the frigid depths of winter. He had a bad feeling about today, one that settled deep in his gut.

When he returned to the worksite, preparing to clear the last bits of debris from the House of Assembly, a hand struck him.

"Are you Taicho of Lornadion?" A man was speaking to him, dressed in black, with the moon necklace of a royal official.

His eyes were dark and questioning. A dagger was buckled to his side, and behind him was a pair of hoplites with blue-crested helmets.

"I— I—" Taicho felt sharing the truth would not be in his interest.

"Come with us," the man said. "You have an invitation to the High City."

Taicho had no choice but to follow.

HIGH CITY, THÉNAI

The High City was the roof of the world, the summit over which the government of Thénai gawked and scowled. Here, on the lofty height, was the Temple of Amara, now shrouded in shadow; the House of the Archon, now the royal household; and the law courts, now open only to those invited. Taicho had been the unfortunate recipient of an "invitation" and as he was dragged their the blood drained from his veins as he saw a military judge seated on a dais. He wore armor over his chest, a bronze breastplate, and his horsehair crest was sideways, in the manner of a high official. A sash of blue was draped over his shoulder, marking his judgeship. In an instant, Taicho knew just what this was all about.

This was what he had hoped for just weeks ago. Now, he was resisting the urge to turn and flee. He would face justice, but in a city changed, in a city completely removed from its old values and ideals. No longer was this a democracy, a bastion of liberty and human freedom, but a monarchy, and living here, Taicho sensed the fear just on the edge of the people's prosperity. What was victory, residing in a place such as this, where its government considered you a "commoner?" How could you share in the joys of a resurgent and dominant Thenoan League when you were ruled over by such people? Rumors had reached Taicho, dark rumors, that the widespread kidnappings and disappearances emanated from here, from the High City, from the city government.

Taicho was led to the military judge, and he knelt before him. He could have died in the siege, in the field of battle. Perhaps, it was here he would die, just after he had a taste of Thénai. It had not tasted nearly as sweet as he thought.

"You are Taicho of Lornadion," the military judge said. His voice was dark and deep. "Your name is on the military register. You were sent to the Battle of Bos, and every member of Nestor's regiment perished. Yet you are here, alive.

"You are hereby notified of your trial for desertion. You shall be sent to City Prison awaiting your day in court, unless you pay the tribunal a sum of five *doukon*."

Five *doukon*! He could not dream of such money. If he had five *doukon* saved up, he would already have left on a ship back home.

"Five *doukon* and you shall be housed in better quarters until the date of your trial," the military judge repeated. "Do you have it, Taicho of Lornadion?"

"No, no," Taicho said, beside himself. "I do not. I am penniless."

"Your trial is set nine days from now, early in the morning," the military judge said. "The Free and Democratic Armies take desertion with utmost seriousness."

"You are not Free and Democratic anymore," Taicho said.

The royal official struck him so fast he didn't see what was coming. A tooth fell loose, and he tasted blood in his mouth. Stunned, he staggered to the ground and collapsed, bruising his hands on the stone of the High City.

The truth was always hard to hear, especially for someone who was not accustomed to hearing it. Taicho did not regret his words at all.

CITY PRISON, THÉNAI

When Taicho was thrown into his cell, he had been stripped to his underclothes, shorn of all his possessions and stripped of his dignity. The anger from his comment lingered, and the royal official had come to watch.

The jailor crudely slapped and iron collar onto his neck, and tied it to the chain in his cell.

The air was cool, and in the crude flagstone, pools of water had gathered in the cracks and crevices. Taicho, weak from hunger, tried his best to accept his fate. Here he would be held, until anyone thought better of it. Here he would wait, until the inevitable trial and the inevitable conviction. Then he would join his grandfather, his great-aunt and his great-uncle in the realm of the dead, floating in pitch blackness in the agony of the River of Souls.

Day faded to night. He was not alone; a dark shape was there, snoring as he slept. For a moment, he thought it was Pythio, though Pythio was long dead.

HIGH CITY, THÉNAI

Against his wishes, Axander had entered the City of Thénai alone. The Oracle had departed for her mountain redoubt, fearing to enter the city bounds. Her instructions had been clear; Theron was to come here, and Axander was to strike him down when he did. Until then, he would be in the company of "Queen" Elena and her silent husband Pereon.

By the time they climbed to the High City, night had fallen over Thénai, and the lights in the streets below formed a bright glow. Queen Elena, ever cold, began ordering her servants this way and that. Then, inexplicably, she left not for her dwelling place, the House of the Archon—now Royal Household—but instead walked in the direction of the temple with her husband. It was Lord Lysander, one of her deputies, who led Axander on his way.

~

The House of the Archon was dimly lit, and candles only faintly pierced the darkness. Down the hallway, Lysander turned. Dark eyes twinkling in the gloom, he said, "Here are your quarters."

The bedroom was sumptuous, though hard to see in the poor illumination: a bed with fine linen sheets, a wardrobe embossed with gold, a Fharese carpet of red and yellow fabric, and a bookshelf packed with hundreds of scrolls.

Axander, as a Kersican, was almost offended at the luxury. From birth, a Kersican boy was meant to sleep on a board, to eat the most meager of fare—including the infamous "black pottage"—and to scorn all creature comforts. He was meant to endure the direst of circumstances; and over the centuries it had served them well. Kersica, for many centuries, had been the strongest city in Eloesus. Now that was fading, he knew… it was fading, and these philosophers and drunkards, who slept on beds such as these, were likely to take control.

He despaired at the thought, looking at the soft sheets, the rug, and the paintings with gold frames: a painting of Ansolon in one corner, and in another, a creature he did not recognize, with three heads, horns and a scaly tail.

"I hope it is to your liking," Lysander said. He shut the door behind him, leaving Axander alone.

Axander got to work, rolling up the Fharese rug and stowing it in the corner, removing the blanket from the bed, turning the paintings inside out to face the wall, and shutting the window so that he would swelter.

When he had stripped to his underclothes, he got on his knees, onto the wooden floor, and did something he had not done in a long time.

He lifted his hands to the heavens. He prayed to Tyros, lord of war: "May you smite me, Tyros, but my heart is not fully in this; I am a Kersican above all things. Destroy these people! Destroy the Thenoan League!"

At his words, he felt a rush he couldn't describe, a lashing out of anger that seemed to pierce his soul.

A scorpion underneath his bed went scurrying out of the room. Tyros would not listen to his prayers.

Here he was, and here he would remain. His mission was not to serve the Thenoan League, nor its king and queen. No, his mission was to slay Theron, hero of the Southron War; to pierce his heart and send him into the underworld. He was only temporary allies with Queen Elena. The war would continue when his task was done.

OUTSIDE THARTA

When the walls of Tharta appeared, bright and blinding, Khloë yanked the reins of Cadelita, stopping her trot. She breathed in deep, attempting to comprehend the city's splendor. She couldn't believe mortal hands had made a wall so immense and towering, with each brick perfectly fitted together, warm in its sun-toned color. For all people said about Tharta fading in relevance, its glory was clear, and the greatness it inherited remained to this day. It was no longer a political player in the Eloesian nation, but what city had walls such as that, etched, as they were, with friezes of the Amazon-Eloesian War, with crystal-white parapets ornately carved at the top. Along the walls were towers, goldish in the sunlight, with red roofs. Yet somehow, the High City in the center of Tharta dwarfed these celestial walls, and on it, the Temple of Alabastros gleamed with blue tiles upon its white marble.

"My gods," Khloë muttered under her breath. "Humans created this city. Humans!"

"Beware," Theron answered. "All is not as it seems. You will know soon that it is just a facade. There is rot setting in. King Gygax is removing its identity."

At the edge of town, they put their horses in the first stable that would take them.

Before the immense Royal Tharta Gate, Theron stowed his lion-skin under a bush, and set his club there along with it.

"Theron," Khloë said. "What are you doing?"

"I must be discreet," Theron said. "We all must be.

"The Oracle's agents are here… even in Tharta. Especially in Tharta."

He looked younger now, like the young man Khloë had known before he had swept her off into a whirlwind of adventure. He was dark-haired and dark-eyed, handsome and swarthy in the sunlight.

She'd had feelings for him before, for a very long time, but she knew they were not shared. She was an amazon, and he a human. It was not meant to be. It was never meant to be.

~

They passed without incident through the Royal Tharta Gate.

The scent of pipesmoke lingered in the city streets. Among the crowds were many women in headscarves and full head-coverings, a polyglot mixture of people from throughout the Middle Sea and beyond; and by the side of the main thoroughfare were many temples in foreign style, with onion domes painted in bright colors or open shrines of black basalt.

In her intelligence reports in the Council of War, Khloë had heard much about Tharta's efforts at "Fharaization," how they had wished to join themselves with the southron world. In an effort to fuse himself with the Fharese Empire, the current King Gygax had married the foreigner Zubeida, and since then he had added two more southron wives to his harem.

Khloë could not make out a single tavern as she passed along the way. The scent of coriander and spice grew as they drew near Tharta's city square. If Gygax wished to irrevocably change his city, to turn it from an Eloesian one into a southron one, he had more than succeeded. The Tharta of prior years was completely gone, replaced, in an instant, with a changed city, one where red-eyed men sat on the street corner and smoked long pipes, where married women covered their hair and the sound of the tamborine and cymbrel was absent. Not a note of music could be heard, and a gloom seemed to have settled over everything and everyone.

The street opened up into Tharta's Royal Square, a vast

piazza which had once been painted in grand colorful tiles, but whose glory had clearly faded. Underneath the feet of the dullards who came and went, purchasing this or that, the reds had turned a shade of ochre, the bright celestial blues a brownish azure, and the brilliant golds a mild yellow. In places, entire tiles were missing, revealing the gravel underneath. The King Gygax had surely joined his people to the Southron World, but he had lost the Eloesian flair for beauty, and did not bother with upkeep.

"How can we find any answers here?" Khloë said.

Theron was silent a while.

For all the countless thousands of people shopping in the Royal Square, it was much more silent than Khloë would expect; though there were shouts of vendors and their buyers, most seem to go this way and that with a singular purpose and not saying much. It was strange to be in an Eloesian city square, the center of civic life, and to hear no laughter, no idle talk and gossip, no music.

"Khloë," he said, "Tharta is neutral ground. If we are discreet, no one will know what we are doing.

"Follow me."

PEACOCK WHARF

Tharta's harbor, now named Peacock Wharf, hugged the edge of the sea.

The smell of fish, late in the day, was almost overpowering. Above-head, seagulls were flying, countless white flocks circling and seeking a bit of dropped bread or whatever humans could muster.

Hundreds of ships were docked in the wharf, but many docks were empty. Here, at the entryway, an old wizened man sat smoking a pipe. His eyes were a bright red, and his face was gaunt. Hunger he had, but the pipe was all he cared for. It would surely waste him away. It would be the end of him.

For the first time, music echoed through the harbor, a soft and silent strain. Just ahead, a man sat playing a lyre in the southron mode. His collection cup was empty. He, also, looked thin. It seemed a malaise had fallen over Tharta, over every soul, every man, woman and child. Khloë herself had begun to feel tired, and wondered if—now, at midday, when the sun was at its hottest—she and Theron should find some public space, lie down, and take a nap.

But Theron pushed ahead, through the crowds, into the harbor below.

Near the edge of the water, a man dropped raw chicken in a vat of oil, and some had lined up ahead of him, coins in hand. Next to him, a man in a turban sat, playing a pipe, as a snake reared its head and danced to the tune.

"What are we doing here?" Khloë said.

"Hush," Theron said. "You will know, soon enough."

It was a matter of days before his words came true, though it seemed like weeks.

Theron and Khloë had taken up lodgings in a seedy inn on the edge of the harbor, eating nothing more than bread and drinking nothing better than watered-down wine.

Old tensions flared once again, and they began to bicker, over this or that, but above all, that Theron refused to tell Khloë anything, of why they had come here to Tharta, and who, or what, they were waiting for.

Soon, word spread through the inn that the King of Tharta was preparing for the Festival of Third Night. Was it already so late in the summer? Word also reached Khloë that one of the kings of Kersepoli had fallen on the field of battle, and the armies of Thénai had begun to press into Kersican territory. To Khloë's wonder, she did not react well to that news, but with despair. She knew that whatever victories the Free and Democratic Armies achieved, "Queen" Elena would be the supreme beneficiary.

Late one afternoon, when the heat was nigh unbearable, and everyone in the inn had left to recline in the outer portico, Theron returned from a long trip and beckoned Khloë. "Follow me," he said.

Khloë got up from her dry bread and weak wine, and gladly followed him.

~

In the streets of the harbor, many denizens did not make use of the lavatories and sewers, but instead flung their refuse from their windows, allowing it to gather and stain the once-white streets. The smell of pipe smoke had once given Khloë a headache, but now she had largely gotten used to it. The scent of refuse, however, was something that could never blend into the background, and as she walked, she felt the nausea rising up once again within her. The city of Tharta, the Royal City, the most ancient and storied in Eloesus, had changed, and not for the better. It had changed for the worse.

Near the sea, up above a stone bulwark, was a table and a set of chairs, shaded from the sun by an immense parasol. The Thartan sun was so bright and glaring she could not make out those who sat on it: two men, inky black silhouettes to her eyes. They were sitting upright, without food or drink. They had been waiting for Theron and Khloë, but who knew for how long?

"Theron," one man's voice she did not recognize. It was deep and resonant.

"Khloë," said another, and she instantly recognized it. Teucer, once the Speaker of the Assembly, was here in Tharta, here with them. It seemed impossible.

"Teucer?" she said, unable to believe her own ears, unable to believe he had come all this way. "What is the meaning of this?"

"Hush, everyone," Theron said. "We can't meet long."

Khloë and Theron joined them underneath the shade of the parasol.

"Who are you?" Khloë said to the hulking tower of a man sitting next to Teucer.

"Mnester," he answered at a whisper, "of the Choros Regiment."

Here he was, a Strategos, a great general of the Free and Democratic Armies—not only that, but commander of the largest military regiment of all. Khloë could not begin to imagine what they had planned.

ROYAL HOUSE, THÉNAI

The days spent in such softness and luxury had begun to seriously wear on Axander. Each bout of sleep in a soft, plushy bed—even without the covers—and each sumptuous feast, drumsticks dripping with grease and bottomless vats of wine—made him feel a little less alert, a little less honorable, and a little less a Kersican. All the ill talk, all the insults directed toward the Thenoans, they were true.

Axander had left his quarters and was walking down the corridor when he heard Elena's voice call after him: "Axander! Axander!"

But he pressed on, needing to get out, needing to run away, needing to leave the softness and luxury behind, needing an escape.

~

Outside on the High City, on the roof overlooking the world below, the air was not as fresh as it was back in Kersica. The smoke of a hundred thousand fires, the black smog of blacksmiths, and the rising scent of refuse marked this place as a great hive of humanity, the largest city in Eloesus and likely the world. To some it was the height of culture, the place to flock to and make something of oneself, but Axander considered it nothing more than a black spot on the ground, and unfortunate creation. Water, pumped in from far away, and ships which every hour arrived at the harbor, full of grain, allowed such a monstrous thing to grow, to develop into a place where hundreds of thousands of people could live together.

It was unnatural, and as Axander walked up to the edge, looking down onto Thénai, he began to question what he was doing, and every decision he had made. He was stuck here among these people, waiting for Theron's supposed return.

He had become a hero, a servant of the Oracle, but he began to look back on his days as a brigand wistfully. There, in idyllic hills and forests, he had spent many years far from habitation, with only his fellow bandits to keep him company. It seemed, despite his new status, that he had been happier back then, though it had been difficult work, and dishonorable work. Now he had to live in this dark spot on the earth, overcrowded and heavy with smoke. Humans were not meant to live in cities; they were meant to wander the fields and mountains. Humans were meant to survive, and nothing more. The ancients did not care about poetry or music or fine wares; they did not decorate their homes with marble statues and gold-bordered portraits. The ancients knew nothing except travail and hard work… and they had been happy. The struggles of modern life had made them miserable, Axander above all.

He turned away from the black spot on the earth, the city of countless thousands of souls. The sun's light had begun to wane, and in the Temple of Amara, there was no illumination. There were no torches to light the sanctuary, and it had struck Axander as odd; but he had been pressured not to venture into the holy temple.

He knew that the famed statue of Amara, depicted as a war maiden with a cuirass and spear of gold, had been shattered to pieces. Thenoans had falsely accused Kersicans of blasphemy and impiety; but it had not been the Kersicans who committed the sacrilege. The southron auxiliary, who had disobeyed orders, committed the crime. But it remained a stain against the Kersican name, a protest-cry throughout the Free and Democratic cities. Though it was false, the accusation had stuck. Kersicans had been branded impious heathens, robbers of temples, defilers of holy places.

And yet here, countless months later, the temple sat dark

and unlit; no one went in or out, save for Queen Elena and her husband on occasion. Axander had been warned against entering, but who could command him to do anything? He was a soldier, a man of war with his own will. Who could stop him if he ignored the orders, and offered a prayer to the holy goddess in her temple? He was a Kersican, by blood a devotee of Tyros lord of war, but all gods in the pantheon were held as sacred.

"Axander! Axander!" Elena's voice was like vinegar on a wound. He turned and saw the black garbed queen walking toward him. "I called after you... I swear you would have heard me."

Axander's gaze turned back to the temple, dark, silent, almost brooding. Back home, even in Kersica, the Temple of Tyros on the High City had been a hive of activity, with priests and priestlings hurrying to and fro, doing this or that, preparing for sacrifices or keeping things clean; and more than that, there had been worshippers, bringing bulls or ewe lambs on feast days, or merely kneeling at the threshold to pray. The Temple of Amara, however, was as empty as it was dark, but what got underneath Axander's skin was its complete silence.

"Axander!" Queen Elena said, and Axander reluctantly diverted his attention. "Are you all right?"

"I am fine," Axander said. "I am always fine."

He began to wistfully think of his brigand days again, the days before he became a hero, a pawn in the Oracle's hand. Those days had been simple, but they had been good.

"Tharta has sent an emissary," Queen Elena continued. "We anticipate his arrival this evening. We are in talks to form an alliance."

Everyone wanted Tharta's help, the one neutral city in the Eloesian nation. They were rich, but they had looked south. "I won't be able to attend," Axander said.

"What do you mean?" Queen Elena snapped.

"I am not your slave, Thenoan," Axander answered.

Queen Elena's eyes bulged; she opened her mouth to say something but stopped herself. At last, she turned in a huff and stormed away.

But it was true, all of it. Axander had no master, no guiding purpose except hunting Theron down, and bringing him like a prized pelt to the Oracle. He was not Thénai's ally, and never would be. Thénai, he would never serve; only Kersica would he ever aid. He was a Kersican; it was in his blood, in his innermost sinews. Thénai remained his enemy.

~

It was dark in the Royal House, and the sound of feasting in the east wing was the only noise. Axander was completely alone. In his too-comfortable room, an oil lamp was burning brightly. No one was watching him; the High City was empty. And his thoughts returned, again, to the Temple of Amara.

There was something so suspicious about the situation, how neither priestess nor priestling could be seen inside, how the commoners were not allowed to ascend and offer their gifts and prayers.

Axander grabbed his sword—why, he did not know—and left through the Royal House's dark, empty corridors. He was completely alone.

The night air was cool and brisk, refreshing after the heat of the day.

As he stood there, outside, with his oil lamp, he began to question what he was doing.

He had been warned; and he had witnessed Elena's cavalier

cruelty firsthand. By herself, she didn't stand a chance against him; but no hero was a match for the thousand hoplites who formed her personal guard.

He shrugged off his doubts, and the growing dread in the pit of his stomach. He walked onward, ignoring his feelings, ignoring his fears, ignoring the tension that built with every step toward Amara's temple.

"Do not go there," Elena had said, and so had many others.

Yet he walked on.

At the threshold before its open doors, he stopped, and took in a deep breath. It was almost as if he had hit a wall, a solid barrier of brick, but it was all in his mind; it was all a reaction to his growing terror.

"Tyros help me," Axander said, and instantly felt as if there were a thousand eyes, peering in from the darkness of the sanctuary.

~

Amara's statue was gone, and so were all its pieces. Axander's sandals splashed in blood as he walked on, and he wanted to retch, but his curiosity propelled him forward.

The walls were red with sacrificial blood, and the ceiling was splashed as well. There was blood, blood, blood, everywhere and on everything. There was enough blood to satisfy a thousand gods for centuries.

Axander staggered back to retch, overcome with revulsion. He vomited onto the floor, into the blood.

He looked up, and saw a statue in the temple, whose dark shape he had not noticed, a figure of bronze with three heads and two sets of wings, with horns on its heads and yellow eyes of crystal which glinted in the lamplight. A foreign god was being honored here, a god perhaps of southron invention.

Axander turned and ran, making footprints in blood as he returned to the Royal House.

He had seen enough. He had witnessed enough. He had to go.

HIGH CITY, THARTA

Khloë followed Theron through the High City.

They were headed to the Temple of Alabastros and its Great Altar.

Theron was holding a lamb in his hands.

He had become more devout in these bygone years, more zealous and purposeful. He believed the gods would help him, that they would aid Mnester and Teucer's plan if he showed them enough reverence.

Khloë wished she had so much faith. She prayed, and offered sacrifices on Third Night, but the gods never answered. Sometimes, she questioned the stories themselves, so far removed were they from her experience, so grand and fanciful. Philosophers claimed there were no gods at all, no beings in highest heaven, and they could be right. But Theron walked, in the light of dusk, the sacrificial animal in hand, the knife prepared. He believed.

Beyond doors of gold, etched in reliefs of the Amazon Eloesian War, and down a silver stair into the sanctuary, Theron and Khloë were led into a realm of splendor, one they could scarcely imagine. Crowded around the sanctuary were various items of gold and silver, pots, urns and jars, ruby-eyed figurines and the accumulated wealth of centuries.

But grandest of all was the statue of Alabastros, his head stretching an astonishing forty feet in height, hewn of bent ivory: a bearded figure, holding a scepter in his right hand and a ball of lightning in his left. Around his white head was a crown studded with dozens of gems. This was the chief of the pantheon, the king of the gods, Alabastros, sitting enthroned in judgment.

Before the titanic statue was an altar of white marble, over which a purple cloth was laid. The area was stained lightly with blood.

A priest stood before the altar, garbed in a robe of gold and azure, with a bronze circlet around his head.

"Come," he said, "and make your offering, and your request."

Khloë looked away as the lamb's blood was spilt. It was hard to witness, even though she'd seen it many times.

For this offering, Theron was hoping for success, that the plot of Mnester and Teucer—insane as it was—might pay off, that against all odds, it would succeed.

~

Night had fallen when they left. They were headed to Thénai, the old fashioned way: by horse.

In the stables of the seaside inn, Khloë took Cadelita by the reins and kissed her on the cheek.

Theron took his Fulminor, a white destrier fit for a hero.

Then they departed.

The streets were quiet, and it seemed after darkness fell, few people were about. Commerce had entirely ceased.

But as Khloë rode, she noted faces peering at them from dark alleys, the glint of eyes in the moonlight. She wondered if they were Maids of Prophecy.

Under her breath, Khloë asked for Amara's aid, that Mnester might succeed where all others had failed.

"Lady in Heaven," Khloë muttered, "guide Mnester's hand. Let Thénai fall."

CITY PRISON, THÉNAI

A Week Later...

Taicho had slipped in and out of consciousness. He had developed a fever, with nothing to keep him warm, and the mash the jailer fed him each morning had begun to sicken him. The water was foul in taste, and the prisoner in the cell next to him would not talk; perhaps he could not talk.

In the darkness he sat there, without a hint of illumination, not sure if he was dreaming or waking.

He had thought about all that had to led to this, the events leading to his imprisonment and now, illness. He had wondered what had gone wrong.

He wondered if perishing in Bos would have been a better fate, but he did not know. If he faced military justice, it likely would have.

Against his wishes, he began to vomit onto the stone floor. His soiled and stained clothes had become itchy and putrid.

He had heard all about Thénai's respect for the dignity of life, but he no longer believed. He no longer believed in the goodness of the Thenoan League, or of any city or nation in the motherland.

Most of all, he wanted to go home, to Lornadion, a village by the sea. If he were to die, he wanted to perish there, to face the jailer's sword in the village square.

The fiddling of keys woke Taicho from his dark thoughts. He looked up and saw the light filtering in, the twinkling of a man's eye in the dimness. He recognized his jailer immediately.

But he was not carrying the bowl of tasteless slop which Taicho had dreaded each morning.

"Taicho of Lornadion," he said, "you have been set free."

"How? Why?" Taicho said.

"Your life-price has been paid," the jailer answered. "It has been paid in full. The Thenoan Treasury has accepted the restitution for desertion.

"We do not normally accept payment for such actions. But three *talents* will aid the war effort."

Three talents! How was it possible? Such an incomprehensible sum was the purview of rich families, of kings, of princes and emperors. Three talents was more than Taicho would make in his lifetime, in a hundred lifetimes.

"Thank you," Taicho sputtered.

"Do not thank me," the jailer said. "Thank your patron."

"My patron?" he said. "Who is my patron?"

"He called himself 'Pythio of Abathon's Garden.'"

The blood drained from Taicho's face. Suddenly, he did not want to leave City Prison. He wondered if it was safe.

Abathon's Garden lay outside the city walls, an area of greenery marked with tombstones and mausoleums.

Surely, it could not be Pythio. Pythio was dead.

How could the dead come to life? How could they re-enter in the world of the living?

Taicho had heard stories of wraiths, raised to life, waking the dead from their agony in the underworld, but wraiths could not pay money; they did not know silver or gold, nor did they care for it.

"How? How?" Taicho began to sputter. Was freedom worth this fear, this unsettled dread growing inside him?

Would Pythio be wrathful at him for living, while he died? Could the dead, returned to life, feel emotion?

He had to leave this place… he had to find out. He had to go to Abathon's Gardens, and find Pythio, if he could. But would he survive the encounter? Ghosts remembered their lives, and took vengeance on those who had wronged them.

It did not matter. He would go to Abathon's Gardens… to face his fears, and to face the friend whom he had lost.

HIGH CITY, THÉNAI

Not long after Axander splashed through the bloody temple, his footprints—left in sandal shapes—had instantly aroused attention.

One evening, at dinner, Queen Elena had made mention of it: "Someone has been where they do not belong."

And Axander knew that suspicion had fallen on him; and moreover, that, hero though he was, he could not overcome all the Free and Democratic forces.

In the evening of one of the following days, Axander approached Queen Elena.

She was behind the temple, in its restored aviary, and adding seed to one of the bird feeders.

"My lady," he said with more deference than she deserved, "I am leaving."

"You are leaving." Elena turned. Her wizened face was darkened by her black hood, but the gleaming gems of her gold crown twinkled in the waning sunlight. "Why is this?"

"Because I will hunt Theron myself," Axander said. "A hero does not lie in wait. A hero fights in the open, in broad daylight, in the fields and mountains. I will face Theron, man-to-man, in combat."

"And how will you find him?" Queen Elena continued.

"I will hunt him down," Axander said. "I will draw him out. I will give him a challenge. And he will answer it. He is a man of war... a man of honor."

Axander did not know, in truth, whether he lied or not. Would he honor his words? Would he seek Theron to kill him, or would he return to brigandage?

Most of all, he wanted to leave this evil place, this defiled temple which hosted the monstrous statue, which was propitiated with blood. The effects of the evil could be felt all around, and underneath the good feelings and increasing wealth of the city, Axander could not help but feel a sense of impending disaster, a sense that things were not right… a tension, building among the people, who were largely ignorant of what went on; but above all, the totality of the sacrilege, reaching unfathomable depths.

"I would advise you not to leave," Queen Elena said. "He is gathering an army outside the city. He does not know we know. He is coming right to you.

"Don't you want to complete your mission? Have you not failed before?"

What had the Oracle told him? He had failed to slay the monster Geon, and now it was widespread knowledge; the Oracle had told her.

"I am sorry," Axander said. "I've made up my mind."

~

His things were few in number, and easily fit into a small pack.

The darkness of this place was overwhelming, but what bothered him above all was the memory of what he had seen, the temple desecrated and honoring a strange god… the blood, the horrid blood.

He would return to Kersica. He would fight Theron openly, without the aid of these monstrous people, without the aid of these fiends. It would be better to face him in a place that was not desecrated, even if his chance of success was much less. This defiled ground was eating away at him, filling him with a gloom and darkness he could not shake, not with wine or food or luxury. Even exercise could not shake the sense he was in an evil place, nor the sense that disaster lurked right around the corner. He had to get out.

Night had fallen when he exited the Royal House. Bearing his sword and his sling, he departed, leaving all the troubles of the prior days behind him. The night was cool, and silent save for the sound of the city below. Yet he felt, despite it all, that he was being watched, that he was not alone.

At the ramp, shapes appeared, dark shapes with horsehair crested helms, shapes he immediately recognized as hoplites. There were several dozen of them, perhaps as many as thirty. In their hands were spears and shields; they were ready for battle.

"What is this?" Axander said.

"You are not to leave," said one of them, evidently a battalion commander.

"Return to your quarters," he continued, "and wait on Queen Elena's command. You may only depart with her permission."

It was a sting to his pride, standing there, knowing he could do nothing. No man could defeat thirty warriors at once, not even a hero. The Kersicans mocked the Free and Democratic soldiers, but they knew in their hearts they fought well, with courage and skill.

Axander sighed.

The darkness would not leave him, not yet. For now, until he saw another opportunity, he would remain.

OUTSIDE THE WALLS OF THÉNAI

Taicho had departed the Lion's Gate with nervousness.

The night was deep and dark, and the stars were shining, and the moon as well, but he could scarcely see.

Just beyond him were some scraggly pines which could easily hide a bandit or a robber.

Taicho, clutching an oil lamp, was an easy target. But he intended to go to Abathon's Gardens, come what may, to seek out Pythio if he was truly there.

He hoped to the gods that a trick was being played on him, that he had been deceived, that somehow, some way, it had not been a mistake… the ghost of Pythio had not returned to wreak his vengeance.

Far in the distance, on a hill, he saw the dark shapes of people sitting down, the ends of their pipes glowing in the night. Pipe-smoking, once exclusively a southron pastime, had recently made headway into the Eloesian world, though it was scorned.

Taicho followed the instructions he'd been given by a passerby, on how to reach Abathon's Garden, but he began to question himself.

Was it worth it to find Abathon's Garden, now, in the darkness of the night?

Still he pressed on, down the dark path, through clumps of pine forest and by drooping cypresses.

Eventually, the noise of the city had faded to nothing.

~

The lights of the High City were still visible when the path ended.

In the dim light of his oil lamp, he could just barely make out the shapes of tombs, some in the shape of gravestones and others in the shape of vast pillared mausoleums. Here, many dozens of people were buried, countless souls rotting away underneath the earth.

Taicho questioned himself again, pausing before the threshold of the graveyard.

Abathon's Garden was fenced in, but the fence had been worn away, and it was bent in places, easily traversable. One door of the gate had broken off, and lay on the ground, covered in rust.

Taicho took a deep breath, uttered a prayer, and entered.

~

The greatest mausoleum was just outside the gateway.

Etched in pillars in the Thenoan style, with three consecutive stories and a red-tiled roof, it was clear it belonged to someone of importance.

The writing on the lintel had eroded, but it was still visible: "King Abathon, son of Abatton, son of Amara."

Clearly, this was old, dating before Thenoan democracy was established. The teachers in Lornadion's village square had spoken about that age, how the kings of Thénai had oppressed their citizens, and the revolutionary Ansolon had seized power at the behest of the people, establishing the popular vote.

But now, Taicho reflected, they had regressed once more. An archon did not reign in Thénai, elected by the people, but instead a queen, and a king. Taicho despaired at the thought. The rights of the people had been trampled upon, yet the term "Free and Democratic Armies" continued, as if in mockery.

Taicho pressed onward, through the tombstones, and

noted that this graveyard was ancient indeed, and a place of burial for some royal dynasty. Even the humbler tombstones marked the interment sites of princes and princelings. In total, perhaps three-hundred souls were entombed in Abathon's Garden. Taicho wondered what had happened to King Abathon and his progeny; in all the exhaustive lessons in Lornadion, he had never heard the name.

Taicho pressed onward. Abathon's Garden was silent, eerily so, and the only noise was those of grasshoppers and crickets, chirping in the night. The night was dark, so dark that the oil lamp seemed almost useless.

Taicho breathed a sigh of relief; there was no wraith hunting him, no angry ghost seeking to right wrongs.

He left, thinking of what he might do, if there was a way to get home, even if he had to walk a thousand miles. He wanted nothing more than to return to Lornadion.

He had almost passed through the gate when a gleam of white reflected in the lamplight.

There, on the ground, obscured by mud, was a necklace with a diamond pendant. He recognized the design, the egret of gold, the eyes of white. It was Pythio's.

CITY SQUARE, THÉNAI

Three Days Later…

Taicho was returning to his labors.

The Royal Assembly, where the House of Assembly had once stood, had progressed significantly. The foundations had been laid, and walls of stone had begun to emerge.

He was halfway through the City Square and its crowds of people when he heard a cry: "Lord Mnester! Lord Mnester!"

HIGH CITY, THÉNAI

Axander watched as the Strategos, one of Thénai's greatest generals, approached.

He had come to give a report, an answer as to whether the Thartan king would join with the Free and Democratic Armies.

He was tall and hulking, a brute of a man, and his breastplate was forged of bronze. Behind him were thousands of hoplites which filtered in behind him, hundreds reaching the High City each minute.

Axander could not recall the Strategos' name. He thought it began with "M." But so many soldiers were upon the High City that Queen Elena, and her husband Pereon, had begun to back away slightly.

Something is not right. Axander could sense it.

The Strategos knelt before her. "My lady, Queen Elena, Queen of the Thenoan Kingdom, our first monarch in four-hundred years… May the gods praise you, O daughter of Amara, O scion of a great house."

His tone was so overdone, it almost seemed like mockery.

His soldiers had begun to encircle the Royal House. Soon, they had blocked the entryway, completely surrounding Axander, Queen Elena, and King Pereon.

"My gods," Queen Elena began to sputter, "what is this?"

"I went to Tharta at your behest, O glorious queen," the Strategos continued. "I have obeyed you like always, Your Royal Highness… you, who rule from far above in your lofty palace, here, high above your kingdom, in the High City, on the roof of the world."

Was he quoting a playwright? Axander swore he had heard those words before.

Axander did not draw his sword for fear of provoking the

soldiers, but he had begun to inch away from Elena and her husband.

Each moment, hundreds more hoplites filled the High City. Untold thousands had arrived, and Elena was at their center.

Axander tried to look for an escape route, a way he might, somehow, slip away and avoid what was coming, but he was trapped; he, Elena and Pereon were surrounded on all sides, and the sound of marching feet was echoing as more and more hoplites ascended the High City. Thousands had already come, and thousands more were coming.

"What is the meaning of this?" Queen Elena cried again. "Depart, Mnester. That is an order. The City of Thénai is a place of peace. It is not a military camp!"

"Ah," Mnester said, kneeling before her, "my great and glorious queen has given a command. How can we disobey her… the Royal One, the daughter of the gods, supreme ruler of the kingdom, who rules by divine right…"

Now it was clear; he was mocking her. No one around Queen Elena had ever dared such an impudent tone. But Mnester had the advantage. At his command were tens of thousands of hoplites.

Clearly he was an important Strategos, one who commanded the loyalty of hundreds of battalions.

The blood had drained from Queen Elena's face; she was white, as white as snow, and her fingers had begun to tremble.

Axander had never seen her afraid before.

Her husband, as weaponless as Queen Elena, was clenching and un-clenching his fist.

Pereon had been a great warrior, but now… now he had no way to defend himself. He was helpless, like a lamb on Third Night. He had no way to defend himself, no way to attack.

"Let's be reasonable!" Pereon said. His voice was deep.

"We can have a rational discussion. Make your demands, and we can consider them. There is no need for violence."

Pereon could not disguise his terror; it dripped from every word.

Axander had never seen him afraid, but he himself had been caught in the middle, caught in the center of this battle for Thénai's future, which he had no stake in.

Mnester stood up and cast his sword aside.

"Elena, for the crime of murdering our democracy, we—the Free and Democratic Armies—sentence you to death." He charged forward and grabbed Elena by the chest. He picked her up as she flailed and screamed. He walked to the edge of the High City, and his soldiers parted. Then, with a great heave, he flung her down, down countless fathoms below, to her death.

Mnester walked back and pointed to Pereon.

"Pereon of Phos, southron, and wicked man, for the crime of defiling the Temple of Amara, and killing the goddess's priests, we condemn you to death by burning. Tonight, you shall face your fate." Mnester's eyes turned to Axander, and Axander shrank back.

"Who is this? Your companion?"

"He is a high ranking official," Pereon said, "Axander, a beloved and trusted servant."

"Kill him!" Mnester barked, and a few dozen Free and Democratic soldiers charged with swords.

Axander drew his blade. It was time for a test, a hero's test. The battle of the ages would be fought here, and the direction of the Wind of Destiny would be decided.

CITY SQUARE, THÉNAI

Taicho had barely returned to the worksite when soldiers, hundreds of them, with blue horsehair crests and blue capes, approached. At first, he thought the mercy of the jailer may have been rescinded, but when he saw how numerous they were, how they were pouring in and overcoming City Square, it was clear they were seizing control of the city, that Thénai was in the process of a coup.

The senior of the hoplites, whose horsehair crest was sideways, pointed to the foreman.

"This project is disbanded!" he barked. "There shall be no Royal Assembly. Law, and order, and democracy, are being restored."

In the three days since he'd been freed, he had managed to save two *thalon* and for the first time, had hope he might return to Lornadion. Now it was squandered; the Free and Democratic Armies had turned on their illiberal and un-democratic queen.

The cause of liberty was returning to the League; but the appalling feeling still did not leave Taicho, the sense that he was in a city doomed.

HIGH CITY, THÉNAI

In the span of ten seconds, Axander cut down three hoplites, piercing one in the chest and smiting two others. He fought recklessly, pushing ahead, trying to make his way toward the ramp that led into the city below.

But he quickly realized it was a pointless endeavor; thousands of hoplites crowded the ramp, and tens of thousands were making there way up. Instead Axander turned and barreled ahead toward the only safe haven available to him: the temple, whose doors were still open.

He slashed, stabbed and smote, charging forward and the ranks of the Free and Democratic Armies began to break. At last, he opened up a path for himself and sprinted into the temple's darkness. Then, with a sword in his left hand and a handhold in his right, he shut the doors, one by one, then—in the darkness—sealed them.

In total darkness, panting and sweating, he began to realize just where he was. He knew that, though he could not see, something was there with him in the sanctuary, an object of forged bronze, on whose account many hundreds of lives had been lost. The smell of putrid blood was everywhere, and wherever Axander walked, he splashed.

All he had to do, now, was find a way out, before they broke through the doors. Then he could run free, and leave the city altogether.

CITY SQUARE, THÉNAI

Not long after the worksite had been disbanded, trumpets began to blow, and the hoplites in the city square began giving orders to common citizens, announcing that the leader of the coup, Mnester, was going to speak.

In the confusion and terror of the attack, many merchants had packed up their stalls and fled, and the sounds of music and revelry had ceased. In fact, a silence predominated, a mystified silence of growing dread. Nonetheless, some citizens did obey, and Taicho was among them, gathering before the dais and its lectern, hoping to glean just what was going on.

~

An hour later, after waiting in the sweltering summer heat, the leader of the coup Mnester appeared. He had removed his helmet, but his sword was at his side.

"People of Thénai," Mnester said. "You have been liberated."

There were a few scattered cheers echoing throughout the crowd, but most were too confused to react. Two others took the stage, one older, wearing a blue-sashed white chiton, and the other younger, with short hair, who had the look of a soldier about him.

"Tomorrow there shall be elections," Mnester said. "Democracy will be restored. For the title of archon, you may choose from two names: Teucer and Gaion. The elections for the House of Assembly will be held next week. Two-hundred positions must be filled."

Yet as hopeful and optimistic as his tone indicated, his words rang hollow. It seemed preposterous, even to Taicho, that things could go back to the way they were, that the fury and debate of democracy could return so suddenly after so long a break. Thénai had been ruled by a king and queen, monarchs who had robbed the treasury and called those underneath them "commoners." How could they forget? How could they return to the liberty of the past, especially with soldiers flooding the streets, and more hoplites arriving by the minute?

INSIDE THE TEMPLE OF KRONOS, THÉNAI

Axander knew the peace couldn't last.

The first blow of the battering ram caused the temple to shudder, and the sound of splitting wood echoed through the hollow sanctuary.

Axander began to splash through the sanctuary, finding his way to an equally dark corridor. There was no way out, no way for him to escape.

He returned to the sanctuary, and braced himself against the door.

The battering ram hit again, but the damage was only slight, and though the temple reverberated, it held firm.

Ten hoplites would endure injuries if they tried to halt such an impact, but Axander remembered he was no normal man. He was a hero, like Phillipidēs or Theron. With effort, he could hold them off for a while; he could prevent them from entering the temple.

The battering ram struck once more, but this time, there was no damage, and Axander, putting all his weight against the door, had halted the blow.

"Oh, Tyros," Axander said, "Tyros help me." And the darkness of the temple seemed to deepen, a darkness not just of the light but also of the soul, and he was more aware than ever of the creature behind him, leering at him from the blackness.

I am not alone.

CITY SQUARE, THÉNAI

Taicho had withdrawn to the square's edges, traumatized and still reeling from the days' events, the loss of his means of income, the increasing hopelessness of ever getting home.

In the light of the streetlamps, his thoughts returned to Pythio and his experience in Abathon's Tomb. He still had the egret necklace; it was safe in his pocket, but he dared not sell it for fear of his friend's vengeful ghost.

The soldiers in City Square had caused most to leave, exiting through the various streets and roads which formed the city's shape. Taicho remained, worried to leave, afraid to go anywhere, and especially fearful to go to sleep, and let his guard down, should disaster come.

The soldiers had built a great platform in City Square, constructed of wooden boards. Toward the center of it, the hoplites began to drag numerous dark figures, figures he recognized by their black robes. One, Taicho recognized as Lysander, the second in command, the senior most official in the royal household, behind only Elena and Pereon.

Taicho's friend from the worksite told him, before he fled City Square, that Queen Elena had been thrown off the High City, and that when she reached the ground, dogs had torn her apart, rending her bit by bit. It was hard to believe, but Taicho couldn't help but feel a bit of joy rising up inside him. Queen Elena was dead! What did it matter how she died, or who had done it.

The hoplites were tying the black-garbed figures to posts. They were going to burn them alive.

Taicho felt sickened. He had waited carefully, not wanting to return home, but this was something he could not witness.

He heard a voice cry out, deep and resonant: "You will regret this!"

Taicho fled City Square as the platform was set alight, and the screams were consumed by the roaring flame.

As he fled, chaos was erupting; on a street corner, he noted two hoplites, both in blue capes and helms, locking arms. Screams rang out in the distance, and the sound of shouting echoed.

Taicho had to get out of Thénai, quickly. He did not know what was coming, but it wasn't good.

INSIDE THE TEMPLE OF KRONOS, THÉNAI

An hour after the battering ram began to bludgeon the door, Axander—still bracing against it—waited for the next blow.

But it did not come. He put his ear to the door, and he heard whispers and murmurs. Soon, there was just silence.

Axander, slumped against the wood, took in a few deep breaths. He did not know when the armies' effort would resume, but for now, he would rest, as much as he was able.

INSIDE THE TEMPLE OF KRONOS, THÉNAI

Axander woke with a start.

He had fallen asleep! How had he fallen asleep? How was it possible?

He was sprawled against the door, partially kneeling in the blood. Outside, there was nothing more than silence, and through the crack in the door, the faint light of dawn was shining, a golden pink color.

They had abandoned the effort, but Axander wondered why.

But he was safe… he had passed the hero's test. He had overcome his enemies, and he had not perished.

He waited a while, not sure what to do. An entire day had passed, and he had awoken fully rested, though he was hungry and thirsty.

He dared push open the door a slight bit, allowing him to peer into the High City.

It was empty, and utterly silent.

He opened it further, then stepped out into the open air. Compared to the foul, stuffy atmosphere of the temple, Axander had entered a garden of freshness, where the winds—blowing down from the mountains of the world—spiraled and swirled. He took in a deep breath, and the sickness of the temple left him. He was free; he had escaped what had befallen Elena and her husband Pereon.

I am a hero. I am truly a hero… like Theron and Phillipidēs before him. He had overcome the Free and Democratic Armies, but they had been distracted… though by what, he did not know.

The law courts were empty, and the windows of the Royal House were dark. The noise from the city below seemed to have lessened.

What had happened in this dark night? Axander was glad to be alive, but he knew that whatever had happened was ominous.

Despite the fact he was alone, Axander drew his sword in his ride hand, and made sure his sling was at the ready. He fixed and then re-fixed his headband. He began to walk, leaving a trail of dark blood by his sandals.

When he reached the edge of the High City, he noted smoke wafting up from a few buildings, and around the City Square, fires that were still smoldering. A battalion of hoplites were marching through City Square in formation, bearing shields and swords.

In the harbor, far off in the distance, separated from the city by the Long Walls, there were ships in the harbor, military ships: triremes and quadremes both, their sails spangled with the gold laurel wreath of the Thenoan League. Yet what Axander did not understand was the quietness of the city, how—despite it being the home of some three-hundred-thousand souls—he did not hear the rattle of chariot-wheels or the sounds of shouting and laughter.

Then he looked beyond the city walls, and saw armies, countless armies, encamped around Thénai. Their standards were not gold and red, like those of the Kersican League; no, they were white and yellow and brown, hundreds upon hundreds, thousands upon thousands, and amid the sheen of armor Axander noted a blue color to the capes and plumes of the helmets. It was not the dark navy blue of the Thenoan army, but a lighter blue, cerulean, the color of the clear sky. What this army was, and whom it entailed, Axander could only guess.

The Free and Democratic Armies had re-captured their town from the king and queen, only to be waylaid by another. Axander had no way of knowing who it was and no way of discovering.

For now, at least, he would remain here, on the High City, where he had a modicum of safety. The Free and Democratic soldiers knew him at worst as a servant of Elena, and at best as a Kersican.

His eyes returned to the darkened temple and the abominable statue that lay within.

He wondered, in his silent and un-molested state, if he could do his part for the holy gods… if he, with the tools available to him, could destroy the foul thing that had taken so many lives. He was not a priest, and he could not re-sanctify defiled ground, but he could remove its source, and pray to the holy gods to forgive the sacrilege.

THE GRAY HOUSE, LAOMER'S STREET, THÉNAI

Huddled in a darkened room, Taicho sat with his friend Namos, a friend he had met from the worksite.

The night's events were still heavy on both their minds, though now they were engaged in a game of chess.

Taicho had placed his Satrap right where he wanted him. There was no way Namos' Padisha could escape.

But Namos moved his Warrior across the board, knocking the Satrap out and, amazingly, putting Taicho's Padisha in checkmate.

"Namos," Taicho said, "you are a magician."

"No," Namos said, "I've just played this game much longer than you."

The rules in this version of chess, called Korthian chess, were different from those in the game people in Lornadion played. But it was no excuse for such an embarrassment; they were similar, after all.

This was how they took their mind off the danger they were in.

They were poor, with no means to escape, and outside, armies had surrounded the city walls.

It was not Kersicans who fought them, nor Korthians or Thartans or southrons.

No; it was the Oracle's army… the Oracle, who had, under the nose of the warring Kersican and Thenoan Leagues, gained a territory of her own, and power that was not just spiritual or mystical but now temporal.

"Why do you think the Oracle is fighting us?" Taicho said.

"I don't know," Namos answered. "Perhaps, because we don't listen to her."

Taicho wondered if it had something to do with the temple. But the temple had been in its state long before Mnester's coup, before he had surprised "Queen" Elena and established the "Thenoan Provisional Government."

The elections were supposed to be held today, but Taicho hadn't seen anyone go to City Square. Most people were too frightened by the siege.

It amazed Taicho that the Oracle had acted so quickly.

In a day, Mnester had seized power, and that very night, the Oracle's armies had arrived. He'd heard people say the Oracle knew the future, but he had never believed it. He, like most people, had considered her a madwoman. Now she was intent on extracting her demands, though Taicho did not know what those demands were.

Now that the armies were Free and Democratic again, Taicho considered joining the ranks, but he found himself staying in place. Perhaps, it was the mystery of what happened to him, how, beyond the grave, someone named "Pythio" had paid his ransom, how he had found an egret necklace just like his outside the city. Perhaps, he was too fearful of the portent and what had occurred.

Taicho reached under his shirt and felt the pendant. It was still there.

"What are you doing?" Namos said.

"I… ehrm…" There was no way else to explain. He removed the necklace of gold and set it on the table. It was glinting in the daylight. "I found this in Abathon's Garden."

"You fool!" Namos cried. "You could sell that for thirty *doukon*. We could be on a ship by morning."

"It's special to me," Taicho answered. "It doesn't belong. The dead are—"

"The dead are in the dirt, rotting away!" Namos said.

"Come, let's go sell it. Or do you want to die?"

"I won't sell it," Taicho answered. "I never will. It belonged to my friend."

His friend was dead, and now tossed about in the River of Souls, condemned to the underworld.

Namos scowled. "You are a fool, Taicho," he said. "A damnable fool."

~

Taicho left the Gray House after the chess game had gone so awry and Namos turned against him.

The memories of the prior night returned to him, the purges in the city square, the mass-murder of everyone in the so-called "royal" administration, the viciousness that almost outstripped Queen Elena at her worst.

As he walked the empty streets, he balked at the thought that democracy, of any kind, had been restored. Hoplites were posted on every street corner, bearing spears and swords. Those that went about their business did so hurriedly, without comment.

It was in this war-torn, besieged city that Taicho lived, a place far removed from the peace and placidity of Lornadion. He wondered how long the city could hold out. The walls were strong, and no doubt many thousands of tonnes of grain had been stored away, but hundreds of thousands lived in Thénai. It was the largest city in the world. There were so many mouths to feed that it was inconceivable the colonies could meet their needs, or that the colonies would be willing to.

Eventually, he reached the harbor, hoping against hope that someone with a charitable heart was headed west, to Dys and Lornadion. He had three *thalon,* coins of copper, clutched in his right hand.

The docks were mostly empty, and warships patrolled the waters far ahead. No sailor was headed to Dys, he learned after some serious inquiries. Instead he walked to the water's edge, and uttered a prayer to Lorenos god of the sea. "Take me home, Wave-Rider," he breathed, and offered all he had, tossing the coins into the waters.

But the wind blew, and clouds began to crowd out the sun. It was almost autumnal, though Third Night was days away.

"Pythio," Taicho said as the waves began to grow in size and crash against the harbor wall. "Pythio, if you are still here, in the world of the living, then speak to me."

THE ROAD

A FABLE

One day, a traveler prepared for a journey to a far country, intending to take the Road to its maximum extent. Many in the city cautioned him against it, but he ignored their pleas.

He started early in the morning, and when he had left the city behind, he was almost stopped by a violent rain. Still, he pressed on.

He continued over the next month, and was waylaid by bandits, robbed of almost everything. Still, he pressed on.

Eventually, after two years' journey, he reached the land of the Anthropophagi. He was attacked, wounded terribly, and almost froze to death in that land of violent ice and snow. Still, he pressed on.

At last, when the traveler was an old man, he passed over the Empyreal River into the land of the gods beyond the North Wind, where there is no winter and no summer, just spring all year long.

He was penniless and wounded, and many asked him there if he would have changed anything. But he said no, for the journey had made him what he was, and he had reached his destination.

—Amalchio

THE SUN KING'S ROAD NEAR THE BORDER OF KERSICA AND THENOA

For many weeks, now, Khloë and Theron had rode at the quickest possible pace.

Theron's plot to overthrow the Thenoan government had gone ahead, but whether it had succeeded, they did not know; they had not heard from anyone traveling along the way, not even those headed westward. As far as Khloë knew, Queen Elena still reigned on her illegitimate throne, and Mnester was still a Strategos with forty-thousand men answering to her.

That night, they stayed at a roadside inn, and it all changed.

In a darkened room lit by the flare of candles, they overheard a merchant speaking, saying that Thénai was besieged, and that none could go in or out and sell their wares.

Khloë pondered to herself, wondering if Queen Elena had discovered the plot, and now Mnester intended to seize the city by force.

"Have we failed?" Khloë said.

"We will know soon enough," Theron uttered quietly.

Khloë's thoughts drifted off. She looked out into the window and saw, in the dimness of the evening, the blasted plains of Kersica. Somewhere out there, far to the west, was the white shore of the sea, and beyond the sea and its tumultuous waves was Amazonia. She wondered, after all this effort, if that was where she truly belonged.

She could feel doom falling over her. The situation in Eloesus had never seemed more hopeless. Her father had taught her that sometimes, when a task grew too difficult, it was best to give up and move on to another. Her father had also warned her against venturing into human lands to seek her fortune. "Amazons do not belong there," he had said. He was a wise man.

~

The summer had reached its fullness when Theron and Khloë, disguising themselves in hoods, passed through the Fortress of Bos which—to their wonderment—was controlled by the Thenoan League and its allies. Much of Kersica had been captured, and though the city that gave the league its namesake was in dire trouble, its territory continued to expand.

She cursed Elena, who no doubt was still reigning as queen. She cursed her for killing Thénai's precious democracy, an experiment in governance which had spread to cities throughout the sea.

Then they reached the hill country of Thenoa and a shepherd—of all people—announced to them that the "false queen was dead."

But who, then, was laying waste to the city of Thénai? Who was besieging it?

HIGH CITY, THÉNAI

Over the days he'd spent on the High City, Axander had been engaged in one of two tasks: fending off the archon's men, who attempted to storm it on occasion, but inevitably fell back; and questioning, back and forth in his mind, whether he should let his guard down and remove the abominable statue from Amara's once-temple.

The High City's ramp provided high ground, enough for a hero to make good use of; but the greatest factor in Axander's survival was the armies' distraction. Engaged in a war of attrition with the Oraclean armies, the archon Teucer sent hoplites with irregularity, and never with full force.

Throughout the course of the week, he'd cut down perhaps two battalions in total. But he knew his position was precarious, and if Teucer ever sent the full force of his troops, Axander would falter.

It was a late summer afternoon and the heat was sweltering. The dusky light painted all in orange and gold. Beyond the walls, the sound of battle had faded; it seemed the sultry weather had sapped even the Oraclean armies' strength.

It was in that dusky light, seeing the calmness around him, that Axander sheathed his sword, took a deep breath and tried—after many hours of alertness—to relax. He turned to the temple. He was hungry, and he thought, after the day's exertion, he might rob its food stores. He had been eating from the larder, nibbling at the preserved remains of sacrifices—pork, beef and mutton—together with the consecrated bread which, without leaven, was still edible weeks after it had been baked.

Besides the temple, the House of the Archon had great food stores underneath it, but its subterranean granary had only flour and grain, and Axander had no time or means to bake.

He always held his breath and tried to look away when he

entered the sanctuary.

The blood, once bright red, which stained the sanctuary walls was now a dark black color.

In the Inner Shrine, which was practically bare, a closet gave way to the larder, a large room where shelves upon shelves of food had been stored: legs of lamb, haunches of suckling pig, and beef ribs, all heavily doused in salt; consecrated bread which the law forbade anyone to eat; and beyond—what was that?—Axander had not noticed another door. He held up his oil lamp and saw hinges, painted over, and the trace of a knob.

He grabbed the knob and yanked, but the door wouldn't budge. At last he kicked, hard, and the door went flying off its hinges. The light of Axander's oil lamp pierced the inky darkness of the room.

The room was full, completely full, of clothing; tunics, leggings, breeches, and chitons alike. When Axander saw that some of them had been stained and cut, he fell backward, sickened at the sight.

Were these sacrificial victims? He didn't want to believe it, but it began to make sense. Elena and her henchmen had been so secretive, so unwilling to let anyone near the temple, and they had gone there at dark hours, after the sun had set.

Nausea was rising up within Axander. He made it a few steps into the larder before he vomited onto the marble. He steadied himself on a shelf. How many lives had that wicked woman taken?

Falling to her death from the High City was far too good a fate for her. Death by burning was too much mercy for her husband.

Axander would destroy that abominable statue; he would

do it tonight, before the sun set. He could not believe humans, or even demons, could be so cruel. And yet they were; all this had really happened. All those lives had been taken. And the blood in the sanctuary was not that of cows, or pigs, or sheep.

The food in the larder had been from a different era, when the temple was consecrated to Amara.

He spared a passing glance at the clothing. "I will avenge you," he promised. "I will avenge you all."

CHAIRON HILL, FOUR MILES FROM THÉNAI

Night had fallen and torches lit up the darkness. The army Theron had amassed, some ten thousand souls, had remained here for weeks, ready to strike.

But Khloë knew, seeing it, that it would not be enough. A vast army had encamped around Thénai, much vaster than this, one which would not easily be dislodged.

Hektor approached them. He was girt in a breastplate and bronze leggings, and a sword was sheathed at his side. He knelt down before Theron, who towered above him on his white charger.

Hektor was not alone. Teucer was there behind him, not dressed for war. He had the white chiton and the blue sash of a government official.

Where Theron and Khloë had traversed the roads from Tharta to Thénai, expending many weeks in the process, Teucer had been borne swiftly away by sea, with his fellow plotter Mnester at his side.

"Rise," Theron said, and Hektor obeyed.

It was still amazing to see Hektor there, a man Khloë had met in a far-off land, one whom she had not thought well of back then. He was not who Khloë thought he had been; he had been an ally of Theron all along.

"Teucer," Theron said.

"*Archon* Teucer," he said. "I won the election. Some three-hundred voted for me."

Khloë could not bring herself to laugh at a moment like this. But she supposed it was not surprising that in a time of such duress, the people of Thénai had failed to vote.

"Have the Free and Democratic Armies turned against each

other?" Theron said. "Do some still recognize the rule of Queen Elena?

"Have they laid waste to their own city in response?"

"Every Free and Democratic soldier, as far as I know, despised her," Teucer said. "The armies encamped around our cities belong to another. I do not know where they've come from or what they want."

Khloë wondered if Old Believers had amassed a great force. Somehow, she was doubtful.

"And the abomination is gone from the temple?" Theron said.

"No," Teucer answered.

"Why not?" Theron's voice had a note of rage Khloë had never witnessed for. "That is your whole purpose! Why did you fail?"

"There is a phantom on the High City, blocking our path," Teucer said. "I cannot redirect all my soldiers when the city's defense is my highest priority. I am sorry, my lord…"

My lord. Even archons called Theron that.

"I will go myself," Theron said. "I'll cut this 'phantom' down if I have to.

"The abomination is not your priority, but it was what was agreed to. It is mine."

"Stay with us," Hektor said. "You are vital to our efforts. There is another army coming… a Free and Democratic one, to break the siege."

"No," Theron said. "I will go, and tear the statue from its place, by myself if I have to."

Khloë put a hand on Theron's shoulder. "Stay with us, Theron. Wait until the city is safe. Then we will do as you wish."

Theron's silence was affirmation. He would not listen to Hektor, or Teucer, or any of his advisors, but he would listen to his friend. He would listen to Khloë the Amazon.

She smiled softly in the dark night.

INSIDE THE TEMPLE OF KRONOS, HIGH CITY, THÉNAI

Axander cinched a rope around the statue's bronze neck. He gathered the rope around his own wrist, and began to pull, hoping to knock it off its platform at its weakest point.

But noise echoed; he turned and saw the forms of hundreds of soldiers pouring up the High City's ramp.

He let go of the rope, grabbed his sword and his sling, and charged out of the temple to meet them.

HIGH CITY, THÉNAI

The night was cool as Axander barreled toward the hoplites, and the moon and the stars were shining brightly.

"Who are you, phantom?" The commander of the hoplites was distinguished by the sideways crest on his helm. "Tell us why you serve Kronos."

Axander sneered at the accusation. Anyone who fought against them, anyone who resisted the unnatural and ineffective concept of "democracy" was branded a demon, or worse. It was the mark of a facile mind, one locked in notions of black and white, and no shades of gray.

"I do not serve Kronos, simpleton." Axander's sword was gleaming in the night. "My purposes are not yours to know.

"But be warned; I am a hero, and the forces of prophecy are behind me."

The commander guffawed. "We will overcome you, 'hero.' You cannot protect your Kronos forever."

It was a summer night, and the full moon was shining. Madness was bound to occur, and people, to act and behave in irrational ways.

Axander sheathed his sword, drew his sling and hurled a stone in the span of a moment.

The commander sank to the ground, skull crushed, and bled upon the High City's stone.

Axander drew his sword and charged, and the battalion broke rank, fleeing haphazardly away, down the ramp and into the silent city below.

THE GRAY HOUSE, LAOMER'S STREET, THÉNAI

For the first night in a while, Taicho was alone.

Namos had fled the city altogether, and others who had boarded in the Gray House had disappeared, one by one, likely following in Namos' footsteps.

Taicho, whose family was on the other side of the sea, had nowhere else to seek refuge, no safer place to hide than the mighty walls of Thénai.

But he could sense the city's doom was near. It was written everywhere, in the way people talked, the low murmurs on the streets, the pall of dread that hung heavy over everything and everyone. Perhaps, this was how the people of Megaris felt when Phillipidēs and the Eloesian army laid siege to it. But life was not so simple and glorious as it was in the Archaic Age and the Megarine War. They had left the golden age behind, and entered one of iron, rot and rust.

The chess board lay on the table, empty and unused, its various pieces scattered and discarded.

Idle, he found himself removing Pythio's egret pendant. He wondered about its significance, if, somehow, the man or woman he'd stolen it from was a great sorcerer or magician.

But more than that, he wondered if Namos had been right, if, after all this, he should sell it and leave on the next ship home.

The dead are in the ground, a famed philosopher once said, *unmoving, unacting, knowing nothing, ignorant of everything.*

Yet how could Taicho sell something that belonged to his friend, one who still caused him great guilt? Axander had spared Taicho. The sight of Pythio's death had moved him to compassion.

Pythio was dead, but Taicho was alive, at least for now, until the Oracle's armies breached the wall. Then the whole city would be doomed, and all would perish, men, women and children. The city would become an inferno, a black spot of destruction, and then a heap of rubble.

White light gleamed in Taicho's window, reflecting on the frosted glass.

Taicho stood up and hurried over.

In the streets below him, far away, was a figure in white, whose clothing was bright and resplendent as the sun. Taicho could not make out who this person was, whether he was Eloesian or foreigner, whether he was hoplite or civilian. But as he looked, the pendant in his hands, which he was still clutching, had grown warm.

~

Taicho followed the figure through the streets of the silent city, like a satyr pursuing a nymph in Themuria.

Taicho was not entirely sure why he was following, but he felt drawn to this figure.

The closer he drew to the creature, the warmer the pendant became.

Through narrow alleys and open squares Taicho ran, into the deep and darkening night. At last, they reached the Long Walls.

Would he lead him into the harbor?

But instead, he stopped, and became so brilliant in his luminescence that Taicho fell backward.

Taicho shielded his eyes with his hands and cried, "Who are you?"

But as quickly as the figure had appeared, he blinked away in a burst of light, and was gone.

Where his feet had been, there were motes of white light,

dying away like embers removed from a fire.

On the street, letters had been etched, burned onto the stone: "Pythio of Strato's Tower."

CHAIRON HILL, FOUR MILES FROM THÉNAI

In the cool of the night, Theron walked away from the camp, leaving his army and his friend Khloë behind him.

A wind was blowing from the east, allowing some of the summer heat to relinquish its grip.

He had commanded everyone to stay behind. He needed time to think. He needed solitude.

Khloë did not understand him, though she thought she did. He had not come back to Thénai for her, or because of her, as she imagined. But he allowed her to keep that delusion. It seemed to make her happy, and happiness was what she needed.

Teucer did not understand everything, or the real cause of the war. He had altered the course of history, and cast the false queen from her great heights, thus erasing her from the threads of destiny. Old Belief would now continue its steady retreat... or so he thought, if he could remove Kronos' statue, and re-sanctify the temple.

Hektor, of all people, knew the most about what was to occur, though not all of it. He knew Theron's motivations, his hidden secrets, his quiet motives. But he was still ignorant of destiny and all its machinations.

He now knew that the Oracle had sent her armies here, to Thénai. "Queen" Elena had been a simple pawn in her hands, but Theron had stolen it from her. Now she wished to seize control of Eloesus by force.

When the camp had become a pinprick of light in the distance, and Theron was truly alone, he knelt at the top of one of the hills and began to pray. He knew what was to happen. He knew, by examining destiny's threads, just what was to occur.

He was ready, but the others were not.

INSIDE THE TEMPLE OF KRONOS, HIGH CITY, THÉNAI

The hoplites had well and left, and Axander, perched by the High City's ramp, had waited for more than an hour. Now, he would return to the task at hand. The abominable statue leered at him from a distance.

He entered the sanctuary, and saw that the rope had fallen loose.

Without hesitation, he tightened it again.

If he tugged on the rope hard enough, the statue would collapse. Cinched fast around its neck, the rope would cause it to give way.

He was sweating, and a sickly feeling had settled into his gut.

Why am I so afraid?

He had to relax, to regain his bearings. This impending panic was consuming him, though he did not know why.

He walked off, out of the temple doors, into the vast openness of the High City.

A great hulking figure was walking toward him. He recognized the creature by its horns, and the gleam of yellow in its eyes.

Lord Skauros was here, having somehow entered the city quietly. Behind him was a pair of Maids of Prophecy. Both of them bore swords.

"My Axander," Skauros said, "servant of the Most High Oracle, we must speak. The holy Woman on the Mount has a word for you."

CHAIRON HILL, FOUR MILES FROM THÉNAI

When Theron returned to the camp, Khloë was nowhere to be seen. Likely, she had retreated into her tent and was sleeping.

Teucer was there, and so was Hektor.

The air seemed to have changed.

For one, Teucer was smiling. Hektor was no longer his somber self.

"Two full armies, my lord," Teucer said. "Two full armies arrive at dawn. We will drive our invaders out of existence.

"The Free and Democratic Armies shall prevail…"

SEA GATE OUTSIDE THE LONG WALLS, THÉNAI

Taicho stared at the writing on the pavestones, trying to stem his anger.

"Pythio of Strato's Tower," the words said.

It felt like he was being toyed with. First "Pythio of Abathon's Garden," next "Pythio of Strato's Tower."

Where would he be led next? And most importantly, was he dreaming? Had he truly seen what he thought he saw?

He pinched himself, and to his alarm, he did not wake up back at the Gray House on Laomer's Street.

Yet despite it all, a hope was rising in him, a good spirit, a beneficial wind. Could Pythio truly be alive?

~

In City Square, a guard was posted, watching over the mostly-empty area silently.

"My good man," Taicho said, "tell me… have you heard of Strato's Tower?"

"Strato's Tower?" the guard said. "Of course. But why do you seek it?"

"My friend is there."

The mighty tower seemed to stretch to the heavens. It was one of many stone towers along the city wall, and high above, on its roof, the blue-and-gold flag of the Thenoan League was flapping in the wind. It was no different from the other towers which surrounded the city, at intervals, along the wall. But this was where

Pythio was… or at least, where he claimed to be.

But a guard was posted there.

"No one may enter," the guard said. "Not even at peacetime. Be on your way…"

He stopped mid-sentence and slumped downward. He began to snore, caught in the midst of a deep sleep.

Taicho rushed through the door, opening it quickly and ducking in. More guards were inside but he sped past them, sprinting up the winding stairwell.

When he reached the highest floor he stopped, breathless, laughing, full of exuberance. A window looked out onto the fields below, and the innumerable soldiers gathered against Thénai. On the floor of the tower was a note.

He picked it up just as the guards pursuing him burst through the door.

"Pythio of Potters' Field!" Taicho shouted. "To Potters' Field we go."

He learned that Potters' Field was none other than a parcel off of Potters' Street. It was once a potters' field in truth, but now, beholding it, he saw it was a warren of buildings, some rebuilt, some still in ruins.

Taicho began to peer through every corner, through every dark alleyway, with an energy he hadn't felt since the day he landed in Thénai, on this accursed shore.

At last, he conceded, seeing no note, no sign of him.

But a voice shouted from above: "Close your eyes!"

He closed his eyes, and a warmth approached him, enveloping him and surrounding him.

"Taicho… friend… I have ascended."

Pythio's voice was clearer than ever.

"I have joined my ancestors in the stars," Pythio continued. "I have become immortal.

"Go… sell that diamond necklace. Board the next ship home."

CHAIRON HILL, FOUR MILES FROM THÉNAI

Theron walked at the head of his army, bearing *Titan's Fist* in his right hand. From behind, with the lion's skin on his head, he appeared to be some creature of myth, with the head of an animal and the body of a hero.

But Khloë, walking just behind him, knew better.

This morning, they would join the Free and Democratic Armies and put an end to the Oracle's power, once and for all.

It seemed almost sacrilegious to embark on this mission. But defeating the Oracle had become everyone's priority , for the Oracle—growing in temporal and not just prophetic power—had besieged an Eloesian city.

Trumpets were blowing from beyond, in the distance, a loud crisp sound, as clear as the dawn.

An hour later, they found the city and its mighty walls undefended.

The gates were open. Teucer was riding toward them on a white horse. "They departed in the night!" He was smiling brightly. "Perhaps, they heard word of our reinforcements. A victory, my Theron, and not a life was lost."

Theron turned to look back at something, though Khloë did not know what. He was not smiling; he looked positively grim.

"And the statue," Theron said, turning back. "Have you gotten rid of it?"

"The statue," Teucer said. "Ah, yes, at once!"

"I will remove it myself," Theron grumbled.

"I will go with you," Khloë said.

"No," Theron said, "I go alone."

"I am following you," Khloë said, "and you can't stop me."

~

Life had returned to normal in the city, free and prosperous, the home of liberty and democracy. In City Square, merchants and vendors had returned to work, selling cattle and pigs, and row after row of late-summer fruits. They were so enraptured that they did not notice Theron walking briskly past them, and Khloë after him, toward the ramp which led to the High City and the defiled temple.

On the summit of the High City, the temple doors were open, revealing the darkness inside.

Theron rushed forward at a sprint, and Khloë charged after him.

In the darkness, Theron laid hold of the statue's neck, preparing to tear it down with his own strength. But he gasped and gargled and staggered backward. Blood was spurting from his chest.

Khloë cried out as Theron fell backward; a great wound had been opened up. And in the darkness, there was the glint of eyes.

A man stood there in a headband, clutching a bloody sword in his left hand. He was smiling, as if he'd just done a great thing.

Khloë was overcome, unable to act, unable think, unable to believe what had happened.

The man in the headband darted away, out of the temple doors.

HIGH CITY, THÉNAI

He had done it! He had finally done it.

He had brought the Hero of the Southron War low.

Axander had such a joy in his heart and a radiance to his countenance, one he'd never felt before. He had never known such success.

Now he was a hero in truth, worthy of Phillipidēs and Helemon.

As he descended from the High City, there were loud shouts coming from up above. He dropped his sword and removed his sling for fear he'd be identified. He could always purchase others. For now, he would depart the city, the city which he despised. He would return to the Oracle to receive his reward.

INSIDE THE TEMPLE OF KRONOS, THÉNAI

Khloë was sobbing uncontrollably. Physicians were coming to tend to her friend, now lying on his back, bleeding profusely.

She cursed the gods for this, for allowing this... for allowing harm to her friend, her love, the Hero of the Southron War.

"Why," she found herself muttering.

But Theron, through his panting and exertion, through all the pain and the life that was leaving his body, he was smiling, a soft, faint smile.

He looked up to Khloë. "Khloë, I am leaving...

"I have done all I can. Now remove the statue! Destroy it! Destroy it before it is too late."

HIGH CITY, THÉNAI

They had to drag Khloë from Theron's corpse. She had kicked and screamed, but a pair of hoplites had finally wrenched her away, away from the sanctuary, away from her friend.

Despite her sobbing, she managed to speak: "Destroy that abomination! Destroy it!"

OUTSIDE THE TEMPLE OF KRONOS, HIGH CITY, THÉNAI

Teucer watched his men as they fastened a rope around the abominable statue.

Then, the three of them walked back and took the rope in their hands. They began to pull.

They yanked and there was no resistance; they tumbled onto their backsides. The rope had become loose.

"Damned fools!" Teucer said. "I'll tie it."

He entered the darkened sanctuary, and the gloom seemed to saturate Teucer's soul. It was as if a thousand people were staring at him from the room's blackened corners, a thousand people wronged, a thousand people taken prematurely to the grave.

He took the rope, now fashioned into a lasso, and tossed it onto one of the statue's three heads. Then he tied the rope tighter, so tight it burned his hands. He walked off a few short feet.

"Pull!" he cried, but there was no answer.

The rope had fallen. His soldiers had abandoned it.

"What is the meaning of this?" Teucer shouted.

He ran out into the High City and caught sight of dozens of people running away.

Then he saw the cause: hundreds of thousands of scorpions, pouring out of High City's pavestone, out of the temple walls and out of the House of the Archon's crevices. They were innumerable. No sooner did Teucer notice this than a harsh sting lit up his leg; he cried out in pain, and hundreds of crawling sensations began to creep up his body.

"Damn you!" Teucer said to the statue, though he knew he'd grown delusional and irrational. "Damn you! I'll knock you over myself."

Wincing from the constant bites, Teucer took hold of the rope and yanked, but the lasso around the statue's neck had, inexplicably, loosened.

Overcome with bites, tears of pain formed in Teucer's eyes as more and more scorpions crawled up his body. He turned off and sprinted away, into the open air of the High City. The bites did not cease, but he continued to flee.

HIGH CITY, THÉNAI

Khloë, kneeling near the body of Theron on the edge of the High City, was overcome with emotion, but even she could not help but spare indignation at the sight: professional soldiers, grown men who were meant to be inured to suffering, fleeing at the sight of scorpions! Surely, they had endured worse than stings.

"I will do as you say," Khloë said to Theron. "I will remove the abomination, even if these cowards will not!"

She charged toward the temple, but when she'd gotten within yards, the mighty doors slammed shut, with a force that amazed her.

Were Old Believers inside the temple? Had they been hidden in there all this time? Were more assassins lurking within?

Braving the stings of the scorpions, she laid hold of the door and tried to yank it open, but it failed to budge. She pulled with all her might, but it was as if the doors had been locked with an iron bar and sealed shut. "Amara!" she cried. "Amara help me!"

The door gave way and she stormed inside, but the stinging of the scorpions became overwhelming, on each part of her body, and she began to fall backward. She fled out the way she had come, and the doors slammed shut once more with a resounding boom.

She ran to the body of Theron and heaved it in her hands. The scorpions fell away from her, as if they were merely defending the temple.

It took three tries to pick him up in her arms, and then only briefly. She would not drag it. She would not despoil the body of a hero, the greatest hero Eloesus had ever known.

Beyond the ramp to the High City, someone was approaching, a creature of blinding light. His face was like lightning, his eyes like flames. Three pairs of wings stretched from his back, glowing white, radiating splendor. Behind him were a dozen women in blue garb and black wigs: priestesses of Amara. Who was this? Who were they? What was going on?

HIGH CITY, THÉNAI

Without a moment's hesitation, Geon charged, and the scorpions scattered before him.

He tore the doors to the temple open, rending them asunder, and they fell inward with a deafening thud.

He hurled the Spear of Pegara and it burst into white flame, a searing javelin of light.

But the statue of Kronos was nowhere to be seen; it had been moved.

Out of the darkness of the temple the statue came running, its body and legs of bronze, its metal eyes emitting a soft glow. In its hand was a trident.

Geon at last fell backward, unarmed, with just the Shield of Pegara to defend himself.

The statue struck him with his trident, and the Shield of Pegara burst into a thousand shards. Unarmed, defenseless, Geon stood stunned, unable to respond, unable to move.

When the trident struck his body, flame answered, and the creature growing inside Geon burst free from its earthly host.

Peace filled him, beautiful peace.

HIGH CITY, THÉNAI

Khloë hugged the body of Theron tight as the unearthly creature erupted into a dazzling burst of fire and lightning. When the smoke cleared, the statue was a bronze puddle, and a creature of pure fire, with wings of flame, was ascending to the clouds.

No, there were two creatures, two beings, drifting upwards, one clinging to the other, one which did not belong.

HIGH CITY, THÉNAI

In the midst of the bronze puddle was a red-scaled worm, writhing and wriggling amid the glowing liquid. Khloë approached with her sabers.

It was like the larvae of some insect, but Khloë knew it was far more dangerous. When she saw its blood-red color, she thought of Kronos, the demon lord, Eloesus' ancient enemy.

With three sharp strikes, she cut the vile creature into sections, and its wriggling ceased. The crimson of its scales faded to a dull, lifeless gray.

Hoplites were pouring into the High City, hundreds of them. Among them was Teucer.

"Khloë," Teucer said. "What has gone on?"

"I don't know," Khloë answered, "I don't rightly know."

THE RUINED TEMPLE, MOUNT OF PROPHECY

Three Months Later…

Axander's journey had ceased.

The temple's white pillars lay in ruins, some collapsed and broken in half, others standing unsteadily.

In the lawn outside the temple, satyrs were reclining with bottles in their hands.

And ahead of Axander, near the temple's stone altar, was the one he sought: Io, the Oracle, the prophetess, the Woman on the Mount.

She was naked, and the snake was coiled next to her, its tongue flaring, its gold eyes twinkling.

Axander staggered forward and fell prostrate before her.

"My master," he said, "I have done as you wished."

From behind one of the pillars, Lord Skauros emerged, bearing an axe in his hand.

From behind another pillar, a Maid of Prophecy emerged, carrying in her hands a bowl.

"One last task is left for you," the Oracle said, "and then your name shall be writ in the history books and remembered for eternity."

Axander looked up. "What is it, my master? Anything… anything for you!"

"Drink deeply of this hemlock," the Oracle said. "I have no more use for heroes, anymore."

Axander stood up, and began to walk backward.

But satyrs were behind him. He was surrounded on all sides.

He had no sword, no sling; he had thrown them both away.

The Maid of Prophecy was approaching with the bowl of poison.

"Drink!" the Oracle said.

"No! No!" Axander replied.

"Then we shall do this the difficult way," the Oracle said.

Lord Skauros charged forward and Axander tried to run. The axe took him in the back of the head.

As he lay there, slumped and bleeding, in his death throes, as his consciousness faded, drums began to play, and pipes. Here on the Mount of Prophecy, here, wherefrom the Wind of Destiny blew, the revel would continue, though heroes would be no more.

THERON'S HERODIUM, OUTSIDE THÉNAI

Thousands had gathered to witness Theron's interment, and not just Thenoans.

Herodota, standing before the coffin, had sprinkled the sacred incense over the wood, and consecrated his body to Amara.

At the front of the crowd of people were the Kings of Kersepoli, King Phaedrion and the newly-named King Perēs. Beside them was King Gygax, his wife Zubeida and Gygax's mother-in-law, frail and wrinkled, wrapped up in a black headdress.

"We gather here to honor the memory of a hero," Herodota said, "a hero in the truest sense of the word. For he sacrificed his life for humanity, and brought peace to Eloesus, and an end to the war.

"Such heroes do not live long. They are here in a flash, and then they are gone. But for all ages, Theron's name will be remembered… the hero of his country, enshrined in this temple tomb."

Theron was not the only loss.

Herodota's friend, the one who had restored her faith and brought healing to her heart, was dead as well. But Geon would not be remembered like Theron. Geon would not want to be remembered. His purposes were far above concerns for the history books, like Phillipidēs said the "imperishable fame."

Geon's herodium would not be built. But his memory would live on in her heart, and in the hearts of Sister Hippolyta and all the junior priestesses.

"As we remember him, let us also honor him," Herodota said. "Let Eloesians never again turn on their brother. Let us remember our agreement of peace."

In the somber crowd, Herodota could not make out the face of Theron's friend. The amazon Khloë was nowhere to be seen.

The signs of autumn were everywhere. A breeze was gently blowing.

It had been a somber day, a somber year, a somber decade. But peace was entering Eloesus, peace that—Herodota hoped— would last for all time.

PORT URSA, JOGHEIRA, AMAZONIA

When Khloë stepped off the boat, Amazonia—her land, her homeland, the place of her birth—seemed at once changed and deeply familiar.

Everything was as it had been. Few sailors went in and out. It was late afternoon, and most fishermen had gone home for the day.

It is I who has changed.

But she did not regret her decision, not even a little bit.

The death of Theron, her friend, had convinced her above all other things that the human world was no place for her. If such a tragedy could occur to someone so undeserving, then, why, what was she doing there? She did not belong. It was here, in the tranquility of Amazonia, in its tiny villages and hamlets, that she belonged.

If she rode quickly, she could get home before sundown.

What would Mother think, and Father? What of her sisters and brothers? Would they still accept her, the prodigal daughter who had left them behind for adventure, and received, in return, heartbreak and loss? There was only one way to find out.

In a stable in the harbor, she rented the service of a pack mule and loaded all her luggage, her clothing, her money, her mementos and memorabilia, onto its pack. Then, with a heavy heart, she set out, away from Port Ursa and down Amazonia's winding roads.

MARKET SQUARE, BYTHIA, JOGHEIRA, AMAZONIA

In the market square, Khloë's sister stood alone, purchasing lettuce from the grocer.

Amid the flat-roofed buildings, amid the scent of tulip and jade and cormoranth, Khloë dropped her bags, and began to weep.

Jessa saw her instantly.

"My sister! My sister!" she cried and rushed over to her, meeting her in an embrace. With her arms wrapped around Khloë she began to weep as well: "My sister! My sister! You've been gone for so long! I was worried you had died."

She had died, in a way. The young girl Jessa knew back then was gone, replaced by a woman who had seen so much, a woman who had lost so much. But she was a woman who was now back home, where she belonged.

"Oh, sister," Khloë said, "do I have a story to tell…"

EPILOGUE

Peregoth Harbor, Western Sea

Many weeks after the journey began, the sailors on *The Sea-God's Trident* finally spotted dry ground.

It was the first port of call after so long on the open sea… Peregoth, a place Taicho had never heard of.

But the harbor amazed him, the marble columns so blindingly white that they glistened in the light of the sun, and in the center of the water a titanic statue of the sun god, forged of bronze, with a crown of rays around his head. The ships in the harbor were innumerable, some triremes, some quadremes, all with red and gold sails and equipped with rams for war. In the city itself, beyond the harbor, which Taicho could clearly see, the soldiers seemed to outnumber civilians, with horsehair crests of red on their helms and crimson half-capes around their shoulders.

Far above, on a high hill, construction cranes were set up, and pillars were being laid. Each moment, oxen ferried more and more pillars to the high hill. They were building a temple!

~

More weeks were spent through the sea, traversing the rough waters, though the sky was clear and blue, and the sun shone brightly.

At last, they reached Lornadion.

Would Mother and Father, and the village elders, accept a coward? He would soon find out.

THE END

THEMIS AND KHLOË

A Story of Themis and Khloë

THE MEETING

Does the world need heroes?

Khloë had pondered the question countless times over the years.

Three summers had passed since she left the human mainland. She could not forget those times abroad, not with all the firewater and feasting in the world.

She was not fond of firewater or feasting, anyway. Firewater hurt your tongue to drink, and it was bound to cause regret.

The fourth summer since she left the human mainland was just beginning, and Khloë was idling in the market square of Bythia. The dog days had not yet begun, but the heat had settled in throughout all of Jogheira and Amazonia.

They were preparing for a festival, the Heracalia, celebrating the tenth year of the reign of the amazon queen Hera.

"Khloë! Khloë! I have someone I want you to meet!"

The voice of Themis distracted Khloë from her ponderings.

Themis was approaching her, a woman two years older than herself, one she had known only passingly in the village during her youth, but now was a friend. Themis was one of the strongest women in the village, and during the annual tug-of-war games, everyone was eager to have her on the team.

Themis, dark eyed, and dark haired, touched her shoulder. "Khloë, you are thirty-three years old. You must be married.

"There is a man… my cousin… not much older than you. I will have you meet him this feast-day."

"Marriage," Khloë said, "I am not sure it is for me…"

Whenever she thought of it, she thought of Theron, the human man she had loved, who had never been wed in his short life, who had perished so quickly, who had burst like starfire and then fizzled away, but who would be known for eternity.

"But I will talk to him, Themis, for your sake," Khloë said.

THE HERACALIA

This Beriotēs was young, much younger than Themis had described.

He was quiet and meek, sitting there at the table, dark skinned, black haired, beautiful. There was a glass of firewater next to him at the table.

Themis was there with him. The music of the Heracalia was in full swing, with pipes and drums, lyres and cascading rhythms.

"Hello, Beriotēs," Khloë said. "May I ask you for a dance?"

~

They danced well into the night, fast, slow, and everything in between. And being with him, Khloë found her reservations, the hard shell she put out to block all feeling, crack and begin to fade. By the end of the night, she was laughing and singing, shouting and screaming.

And when the villagers had all gone home, and the musicians departed, it was Khloë and Beriotēs standing there by themselves, holding hands.

Out of the darkness, Themis and her husband Horēs emerged, both smiling.

"Khloë and Beriotēs," Themis said, "we are spending tomorrow in the mountains. Will you come along?"

KHLOË'S DREAM

The mountains outside Bythia were not mountains in the truest sense. If Theron saw the rocky hills, without a wit of snow, he would have laughed.

But mountains they were to the amazons of Bythia, and Khloë and Beriotēs were hiking through them. Khloë had begun to wonder if this was the man she would marry.

Near the peak of Black Mountain, Themis and Horēs set up camp. They built a fire and began to sear fish which Beriotēs had caught in a creek further down the way.

As the full moon arose, wisped by clouds, Khloë thought again of Theron, the man she had loved, now joining the countless millions in the grave.

She went to bed with a full stomach.

~

Her dream was vivid, more vivid than any dream she had ever had, more vivid than any dream she would ever see again.

Theron was there upon a green hill, a hill whose grass was so vibrant and healthy it almost seemed to glow. The sun was shining on the lion's skin he wore, and his club was in his hands.

He began to pitch back the club, though there was no enemy.

Beyond, satyrs and centaurs bounded through the verdant fields and mountains. Phillipidēs and Helēmon were in the distance, eating berries of paradise.

But Theron was the most glorious of all, Theron in his lion's skin, Therön, the hero of the Southron War. He had been enshrined in splendor.

Theron began to run, and the centaur Aigon met him,

galloping alongside.

In the hall of heroes Theron would feast. In the field of heroes he would fight, and rise again.

Theron had died. Theron had achieved victory. Theron, the hero of the Southron War, had ascended.

THE DEATH OF BAT ZOR

When Bat Zor, queen mother of Tharta, was on her deathbed, her son-in-law Gygax and her daughter Zubeida were not there.

Old and wizened, straining to breathe, she lay upon the linen, overcome with vision and delusion, overwhelmed with images of the future.

She saw Tharta burning; she saw its temples turned to rubble, its walls cast down brick by brick. She saw its fields sown with salt, so that it could not rise again.

But above all she saw a beast with iron claws, more vivid than ever, rising out of the sea, growing so large and mighty that it threatened the world, forming a shadow out of the west.

The Eloesian cities, in the ensuing years, held fast to the Peace of Thénai, never warring among themselves on the mainland. In time, the memories of Theron passed into legend, and many began to doubt the stories of his exploits entirely.

The amazon nation continued to recede, even as the Eloesian cities formed kingdoms and gained great honor.

We Eloesians are scattered across the sea like frogs around a pond. We are far apart and yet close... close, and yet divided. We have settled over all the world and founded cities to glorify the nation's name. Though wars will be fought until the end of our history, let us never forget that we are of one blood.

We are lizards—no, crocodiles of the Khazan! We will always be free.

—Calaïs, national historian, 256 Y.E.

GLOSSARY

CALENDAR

1: *Alphaios* (March)
2: *Pheidos* (April)
3: *Dektros* (May)
4: *Soloön* (June)
5: *Tyron* (July)
6: *Amaron* (August)
7: *Ergon* (September)
8: *Nichion* (October)
9: *Phimetron* (November)
10: *Kryon* (December)
11: *Titanion* (January)
12: *Etapion* (February)

CURRENCY

Thalos: A small silver coin, worth one-fourth a *doukos*. Plural *thalon*.
Doukos: The standard silver coin across Eloesus. It takes many forms but generally has the city's patron god cast onto the front and the victory laurel wreath on the back. Plural *doukon*. One *doukos* is about the daily wage of a skilled laborer.
Oros: A gold coin, worth fifty *doukon*. Plural *orhon*.
Talent: A unit of measurement, worth one-thousand *doukon*.

TERMS

Alabastros: The king of the gods in the Eloesian pantheon. He is revered especially by the Thartans. As king of the gods, he is considered to preside over kingship, leadership, and royalty. He is often depicted as a wise old man. His favored animal is the lion.

Amara: The goddess of motherly love in the Eloesian pantheon. In Thénai and the Amazonian Isles, she is also the goddess of wisdom and battle. Although a mother, she is a virgin. Eloesian legend states she is the daughter of Alabastros and the Earth. Her brother is Tyros, god of war.

Amazons, the: A race of people living in the coastal islands off the Eloesian shore. Their women are far stronger and—some argue—more intelligent than their men. Though they look similar to humans, amazons and humans cannot breed. The child of an amazon and a human is always stillborn.

Amazonia: A term for amazon lands. Amazonia encompasses the islands of Jogheira, Straiteira, Agathe, Kalormene and a few smaller islands.

Ansolon: The founder of the Thenoan democracy and perhaps all democracies. He led a popular revolt against the tyrant king and seized power over the government.

Archaic Age: A period considered to have ended three-hundred years prior to the events of "A Hero's Calling," after which followed a period of chaos, war and widespread destruction. It is remembered as a golden age of heroism. Eloesus' most famous hero, Phillipidēs, belonged to this time period, as did the Megarine War he fought in.

Arkadion: A town, the largest settlement in the wilds of Themuria, called the Bride of the Wilderness. It is a subject state of the Oraclean Kingdom.

Anthropophagi: According to ancient legend, a tribe of monstrous creatures who live in the far north, in a land where it is winter all year round and the snow never thaws. They were said to have one enormous eye in the center of their head, short legs, and oversized arms.

Black Pottage: A kind of gruel that is served in Kersican mess halls among its military. Though none are certain of its recipe, it is infamous across Eloesus, a point of jokes and disparagement. The notoriously foul mixture is believed to instill strength and persverence in Kersican soldiers.

Brecko: The god of pleasure, wine and theater, as well as shepherds. His worship is centered in Arkadion in Themuria. He is depicted as a man with goat legs, like a satyr, but without their furry mane or pointed ears. He is considered the father of the satyrs. The panther is considered his sacred animal, though panthers do not live in Themuria. According to legend, Brecko's mother, Amara, was tricked by the goddess Nix into mating with a goat.

Cadelara: The goddess of horses. Though not prominent in the Eloesian pantheon, she has a significant presence in the nation.

Chess: A game originally played in southron lands that has spread throughout the world. Individual cities in Eloesus often have their own takes on the game, developing traditions of Korthian chess and Thartan chess.

Chosen, the: The most elite Kersepolan hoplites, chosen by the king. Their number has varied throughout history, but is usually close to five hundred. As an elite force, they conduct special missions on behalf of the Kersepolan state.

Civic gods: The gods considered sacred to a particular city. Tharta favors Alabastros; Korthos, Nix and Arephon; Kersepoli, Tyros lord of war; and Thénai, Amara.

Dys: A land far west from Eloesus across the sea, on the border of the ocean, little known and little explored. Thartan settlers planted cities along its western and southern coasts: Mageios, Lornadion, and Agathion.

Fharas: A vast empire, by far the strongest power in the world. It is ruled by the King of Kings, who is considered a living god. The word Fharas and Fharese also refers to a certain region and people—the heartland where the empire began.

Fields of Paradise: According to Eloesian religion, a region of heaven where the heroes and certain virtuous mortals go after death.

Harem: In Fharas, among the Great Lords and high-ranking officials, the separate living quarters for wives.

Herodium: In Eloesus, a shrine built specifically for heroes as well as semi-divine demigods. The greatest of the herodiums is in Tharta, honoring Phillipides.

Hordo: The wife of Ansolon, the founder of democracy. She was considered a revolutionary in her own right, perhaps the guiding force behind her husband's actions.

Hoplite: The traditional soldier in the Eloesian army. Each hoplite has a helmet and a breastplate, a spear and a shortsword, in addition to an iron-rimmed wooden shield. When fighting, he locks shields with his fellow hoplites, forming an impenetrable wall as long as he holds formation.

Kersepoli: A large city, one of the four greatest in Eloesus. It is the most militaristic of the Eloesian cities and is ruled by two kings, either of whom may overrule the other.

Kersican League: A union of Eloesian city-states with Kersepoli as the head. Megaris and the Ten Cities announced their membership within months of the Southron War's ending; a small handful of other cities in mainland Eloesus also joined.

Korthos: A large city, one of the four greatest in Eloesus. It is ruled by an Assembly, elected by the people, and an archon, elected by the Assembly.

Lorenos: The god of the sea, not considered a member of the Eloesian pantheon. However, he does have some temples in the colonies, especially in islands and in the cities of Dys.

Megarine War, the: An ancient conflict, shrouded in myth and legend, between the cities of Tharta and Megaris. According to ancient tales, the king of Megaris Sosimon fell in love with Prophylaia, the queen of Tharta. Sosimon abducted Prophylaia and the king of Tharta declared war.

Nemesis: In Eloesian mythology, the servant of the gods who carries out their justice.

Nix: The goddess of secrets and whispers, her followers call her the Gray Lady or the Queen of Sorcery. She presides over the knowledge of herbs—healing and poisonous—as well as hidden knowledge, wisdom, and the metals iron and silver. She is feared throughout Eloesus, though her name is invoked for protection from the unquiet dead. Korthos was historically the center of her worship. Her favored animals are the owl and the dog. According to Eloesian legend, she is the daughter of Tyros, god of war, and Seladora, goddess of nature. She was hated by her parents and cast out of the household.

Oraclean Kingdom: The most recent political division of Eloesus, an absolute monarchy ruled by the Oracle. Her power extends over the entire mountain region, with its seat of power in the Mount of Prophecy and its largest town, the city of Arkadion. The Oracle seized the land from the Thenoan League, to which the region was once allied, and the Thenoan League—distracted by war, and not valuing the largely barren land—has for now allowed her to operate without resistance.

River of Souls, the: According to Eloesian legend, a river which winds its way through the underworld, carrying the shades of the dead. These shades, neither great and heroic enough to enter the Fields of Paradise nor wicked enough to suffer in the Lake of Fire, float through the river in silent sadness.

Rhegia: A mythical city, said to be the old capital of the amazons at the time of the human conquest. According to legend, the city of Tharta was built on its burnt-out ruins.

Return of the Gods: In Eloesian religion, the time, at the end of the world, when the gods return to their creation to pronounce judgment and bring in an eternal golden age.

Strato's Tower: A large tower near the city gate of Thénai, one of many defensive fortifications along the city wall. It was named for its architect, Strato.

Tigris: The largest city of the Amazons, having about thirty thousand residents plus half as many slaves. It is located on the island of Jogheira. The amazon queen, Daphne, rules from here.

Tharta: A great city, considered the chief in Eloesus. It is ruled by a king but has certain limited forms of democracy.

Thénai: A large city, one of the four greatest in Eloesus. It is ruled by an Assembly, elected by the people, and an archon, elected by the Assembly.

Thenoan League: A union of Eloesian city-states with members across the Middle Sea. The headquarters of the League is in Thénai, where the League treasury is located and all League decisions are made.

Triton: According to legend, an aquatic creature which dwells in the deepest part of the Middle Sea. It has a lobster-like lower body, pincers and several rows of arms. It is said to be the beloved creation and the messenger of Lorenos, god of the sea.

Tyros: The god of war. He is revered in Kersepoli and Isteros; yet he is viewed as never favoring one city over the other, delighting only in battle itself and spilled blood. According to Eloesian legend, he was the son of Alabastros and the Earth. His sister is Amara and his daughter is Nix, whom he hates.

Yule: A holiday common among humans, occurring on the winter solstice. Its origins are obscure, but common features include the lighting of candles and the giving of gifts.

ABOUT THE AUTHOR

Cursed at birth with a wild imagination, Andrew Cooper spent his youth dreaming of worlds more exciting than Earth.

He is a graduate of the Odyssey Writing Workshop. His stories have appeared in Morpheus Tales, Fear and Trembling, Residential Aliens and Mindflights, among others.

CONTACT THE AUTHOR

Visit **www.aj-cooper.com** to sign up for the newsletter and stay up-to-date on new releases.

Find him on Facebook at:

www.facebook.com/AJCooperauthor